# MURDER BETWEEN THE STACKS

A MILLER'S MAGICAL MYSTERY

BOOK TWO

ELOISE EVERHART

ALORIUM PUBLISHING

PB ISBN: 978-1-962759-10-6

Author: Eloise Everhart

Editors: Rashida Breen and Sarah Carleton

Cover design by GetCovers

# CHAPTER 1

Sweat trickled down my spine as I tromped through the darkened building. The sun had finally set, but the heat hadn't dissipated. Instead, the humidity held it in place, making the air in the abandoned mansion cloying. The greater Seattle area had always been humid, but Whidbey Island was usually much drier. The recent storms had settled over the town, making it unusually muggy for the season. I followed behind Sheriff Chris Harris, the beams from our flashlights bouncing off the graffiti-splattered walls.

"The bank foreclosed on the place last year after Harold Mitchell was arrested," Chris said over his shoulder. "The company they hired to do periodic checks on the place called it in. The circle is in the in-ground pool."

"And you're sure it's a ritual circle this time?" I asked.

Chris snorted. "No. But as much as Edgar dislikes you being in this position, he dislikes the idea of you not doing your job even more. It's probably nothing."

*Again.* Ever since I had been hired to the position of liaison between the Wardens of the West and the town council, Edgar Graves, one of the city councilors, had made it his mission to make the position as miserable as possible. Part of my official duties was to look into every crime in the city that could have a supernatural element and determine if it needed to be resolved by the town sheriff or by the Wardens, the secret law enforcement for the supernatural community. As part of the town council, he was allowed to know about their existence. He didn't like them—nor, by extension, me. This was the third ritual circle I had been called out to this week alone, and thus far, they had been graffiti, spilled paint, and an art project a ten-year-old was working on for their mother. Being the town's resident witch expert was exhausting.

We came to a stop at French doors leading to a sunroom. I squinted through the fogged-over glass. The humidity inside was even worse than in the rest of the house. I pushed through the doors, my body sagging from the increased heat.

"The property manager found it?" I asked.

Chris shook his head. "An employee labeling the photos noticed it today. It might have been out here for weeks for all we know. They only do the inspections once a month, and they're a little behind in putting together the reports for the bank."

I swept my flashlight around the space, taking in my surroundings. Half the windows in the sunroom were cracked. A large branch, probably blown in there by a freak windstorm two weeks ago, jutted through an opening in the roof. Broken furniture lay scattered in heaps in the corner. The beam of light bounced off an animal's eyes. Whatever it was skittered away. It was a bit too big to be a rat but moved too quickly to be a possum. *A raccoon maybe?*

I blew a damp strand of hair out of my face, and trudged to the edge of the pool. The ladder was still in decent shape. "I'll get to it, then."

The metal ladder groaned under my weight as I

descended. I dropped down the last few feet. Fortunately, the pool was completely dry. I inched myself away from the wall and prowled around the corners of the pool before circling inward toward the center. I paused at the first sign of a ritual circle. I knelt down and touched it. The circle was dry. I scraped at it with my fingernail, and a fleck of paint came up. While the circle was white, it was clearly spray-painted on. The circle itself wasn't meaningful in any way.

Standing, I swung my flashlight, tracing the lines of the circle. It was a crude pentagram with candles at the points. I grumbled. I would have traded every magical mystery in Point Pleasant for the sound of Gertie, my dairy-cow familiar, chewing cud in the barn right now. At least cows never left pentagrams in swimming pools.

I crept to the first candle and lifted it. *Battery powered?* I set it back down and continued my inspection. I found crystals next, but there was no rhyme or reason to their placement or the crystals being used. Smokey quartz sat next to clear, which didn't make sense from a mystical perspective. It was more artistic than anything. I flinched as a bottle bounced away from my foot, the glass clinking loudly against the cement. I padded over and picked it up. Beer—and not just any beer but a brand I recognized from my high school days, cheap enough for underage kids to buy but fancy enough to impress the girls.

I dropped the bottle and did one final sweep of the space. Relaxing my eyes, I pulled my magic to the surface and scanned the area to confirm what my brain was already telling me—there was nothing magical about this place.

"Anything?" Chris called down.

"Nope." I returned to the ladder and hauled myself up. "Looks like kids messing around."

Chris helped me up the last few feet, and we walked back outside in silence. The night air felt cooler against my skin, carrying the distant scent of wet grass and salt. For a second, I pretended I was already back on the farm.

He fished a bottle of water out of the trunk of his SUV and handed it to me. "Any luck getting city council to switch you to hourly?"

I shook my head as I guzzled it down. My shoulders loosened now that the answer was clear. Fake magic was irritating, but at least it meant I'd get to go home at a reasonable hour. My liaison position had made my schedule chaotic. Some days, I wasn't called out for anything. But on others, I was up at four in the morning and crawling back into bed almost twenty-four hours later, just after three o'clock. Every day was different. It was hard to plan around.

"I almost regret pushing you to take on this role. It's more work than I anticipated," he said.

Gertie was none too pleased with me being away from home so often. I'd missed evening feed time more than once, and I would probably owe her an apple or two to make peace. But whenever I questioned if this was worth it, the faces of the local werewolves flashed through my mind. If I hadn't been involved in that first case, the wrong person could have been arrested. The supernatural community was counting on me to have their backs since the Wardens were notorious for going with the easy answer.

I shook my head. "Don't be. Someone's got to do it. Might as well be me."

Chris squeezed my shoulder. "You're one of the good ones."

I grabbed the clipboard from my truck and filled out the incident report while he waited. I made sure to press down hard enough that my handwriting would transfer down to the two layers of carbonless copy paper underneath. Every incident report had to be filled out in triplicate, one for the city council, one for the Wardens, and one for the sheriff's department. I checked the box at the top indicating it was a mundane case—not preternatural, the term the city council had adopted for the supernatural community.

I was jotting down the last of my thoughts when my phone rang in my pocket. I fished it out as I continued to write. "This is Megan." Over the past few months, I had adopted Miranda's strange way of answering the phone after routinely having to spend the first minute of every call clarifying who I was to whichever department downtown was reaching out to me.

"Hi, Megan." Victor sounded as tired as I felt. "Sorry for calling so late. Hopefully, I didn't wake you."

"Nope. I'm out at the old Mitchell estate. What can I do for you?" I signed the bottom of the form.

"I… there's been a murder at Harborlight Books. Would you mind coming by to take a look?" Victor was the local medical examiner. Like Chris, he was obligated to inform me if he encountered anything strange.

I pinched the bridge of my nose. At this rate, I wasn't going to make it home until after midnight. My new duties as the Wardens' liaison had required me to take on Lindsey —my coven mate Kim's daughter—part-time at the farm. Once the school year let out for the summer, she had agreed to work full-time so I could catch up on maintenance around the farm. I only had her for a few more months before she went off to college. I would have to figure something else out soon if I was going to keep balancing these two roles.

"I'll be right there. Give me thirty minutes." I shoved my phone into my pocket and ripped off the top copy of the form then handed it to Chris and climbed into my truck. Yawning, I tossed the clipboard onto the passenger seat.

"Got another case to look at?" Chris asked, leaning against my truck door.

"A murder at Harborlight Books."

He nodded. "It should be a quick one for you, then. I was

there soon after it got called in. It looked like a standard B and E gone wrong."

I smiled at him weakly. "Who was the victim?"

"The owner."

My eyes watered. I had met the man a handful of times in passing, and he'd always been pleasant enough. Since Avery, I had looked at two other deaths but neither one ended up on my desk. Victor's call was different than the others—I had met the victim before.

Chris tapped his knuckles against the roof of my truck. "Let me grab you a muffin real quick. Dani would be disappointed in me if I let you leave without refueling you."

Dani, another member of my coven, had married Chris just two months before. Having witnessed his wife overcast magic on more than one occasion, he was well-versed in what we needed to keep our magic properly fueled—food. While Dani preferred protein bars and Kim was partial to trail mix and jerky, I had a sweet tooth and wanted my extra energy to come from tasty things. My go-to easy snack was a Snickers, but I would never turn down a muffin or other baked good. Especially since I was pretty sure this muffin had been made by the fourth, and last, member of my coven —the only nonwitch, Heather. While she didn't have magic, she was the heart and soul of the group.

My mouth watered as he returned. *Muffin* didn't do the delectable item justice. It was a triple-chocolate monstrosity with a gooey center.

I groaned as I bit into it. "Thank you. You are a god amongst men."

He barked out a laugh. "Drive safe."

I chowed down on the muffin as I backed out of the driveway and drove into town. The past two months had been exhausting in a way that I was unprepared for. Almost every day, I'd been called out yet another false alarm. Each one required me to check it out with magic. I hadn't ever cast so many spells in such a short period of time. I was getting better at keeping up my magical stamina, but between attending to my liaison duties and keeping my farm going, I was running myself ragged. I stifled another yawn and turned off onto the road leading to the bookstore and the latest crime scene for me to clear.

# CHAPTER 2

I pulled to a stop outside the Harborlight Bookstore and peered out my window at the tall structure. An old lighthouse at the edge of town had been converted into a bookstore about a decade before. At the time, there were only a few businesses nearby, but the town had expanded, and the store was now nestled in a bustling area. All the buildings nearby had a similarly artsy vibe. Most were either newer constructions or had been remodeled recently in Mayor Steven Bishop's campaign to revive the town. The bookstore looked old in comparison. It felt like a place filled with history and with an edge of refinement. That was probably why the store hadn't been updated yet. Everything about the structure was beautifully maintained, including the light at the top that bathed the street in a warm glow.

I hopped down from my truck and ambled to the door. My fingers worked quickly to tidy my hair and smooth down my blouse as I stopped. I hopped from foot to foot to slip boot covers onto my shoes and then let myself in.

The inside of the bookstore had just as much character as the exterior. The walls were exposed brick with warm wood highlights. Handcrafted shelves followed the curve of the walls perfectly. The center was taken up by a massive circular desk where the proprietor sold his wares. To the left was a staircase that rose to the next level—where there were reading rooms—and higher still to an area where private collectors purchased rare books.

I'd been in the store a few times over the past couple of months, and on every visit, it had been immaculate, every book in its place. Today, the floor was a chaotic mess. My gaze bounced between the spilled books and the blood splatter across the back wall. Entire shelves had been knocked loose. The local art prints that were usually stacked at the edge of the desk lay scattered across the floor. Whatever had happened here had been violent. Harborlight had always felt like a sanctuary—warm wood, quiet corners, the soft rustle of pages turning. Seeing it like this was like a punch to the heart. Somewhere beneath the blood and broken shelves, I could still picture the glow of reading lamps and the way the lighthouse windows caught the afternoon sun.

I let out a breath as I relaxed my eyes and looked at the scene through a magical lens. I wobbled on my feet as I turned slowly in place, my eyes sweeping the space in search of magical residue.

There was none.

I released the tension in my shoulders and padded through the room to examine the rest of it. The wood of the shelves was splintered in a way that reminded me of the time I'd had to demolish my kitchen after a particularly bad winter had frozen my pipes and water had sprayed everywhere. It was harsh to look at but wasn't outside the realm of a normal person's strength.

"Is anyone here?" I asked in a raised voice.

I strained my ears, listening for a response. When none came, I continued on with the next steps of my inspection. I muttered the words to a spell that would heighten my senses.

My magic took the form of a swirl of translucent petals that flew out of my mouth and settled over my skin. Only magic users could see the petals, but I still had to be careful in public with spells like that because the effects were obvious.

Divination wasn't my strong suit. Transformation was. I started by heightening my sense of sight, using my limited shapeshifting ability to change my eyeballs from my own into those of an animal. The sensation was strange as they morphed into a new shape inside my skull.

"What on earth?" Victor spluttered.

My head jerked toward the balcony above me, where he was leaning. My hands became clammy, and my mouth went dry as I took him in. His Regency-era waistcoat was rumpled, and his normally slicked-back white pompadour hung loosely over his forehead. His mouth hung open as he stared back at me. While I'd never seen myself when I shifted my eyes into those of a mantis shrimp, I couldn't imagine it looked anything other than horrific. I dispelled the magic, and my body returned to normal.

I gestured weakly toward my face. "Mantis shrimp—"

"Can see sixteen different colors and even see UV light." He blinked and smiled. "That's brilliant. Did you find anything?"

I glanced around the room again. I'd only had access to the mantis shrimp vision for a few seconds, but nothing had stood out. Clearing my throat, I shook my head. "I was going to check scent next."

He shuffled down the stairs and came to a stop next to me. "What do you do for sense of smell?"

My mind went blank. If I had been alone, I would have called on the animal with the best sense of smell out there—the elephant. But I couldn't deal with Victor seeing me with a trunk so soon after the alien-looking mantis eyes. I settled on an animal that would be easier to hide with my hair.

"Bears. They have a really good sense of smell."

"So you'll…?"

I nodded and kept my expression blank, hoping my anxiety didn't bleed through into my eyes. It was painful letting others see how I was feeling. Dani could always pick up on it, but determining people's emotions was part of her divination magical specialty. I relied more firmly on my mastery of enchantment and transmutation magic. The only way I knew how to consistently improve my senses was by transforming part of myself into an animal, which didn't make the process any less embarrassing.

*How can he take me seriously with weird animal features?* I stepped away from Victor and lowered my head to cover my face with my hair as I began the next spell.

The scent of blood hit me first. It reminded me of new pennies. I inhaled deeply, trying to find something under it. The books came next. Paperbacks had a unique scent, sweet and musty at the same time. I shuffled forward, sniffing at the air as I moved. There was a faint floral scent. I couldn't tell if it was shampoo or old perfume that lingered long after the wearer had gone. And under all of that was something sweeter but with a slight hint of ammonia. The cat.

"Where's the shop cat?" I asked.

Victor inched toward me. "She's upstairs."

I released the spell over my nose. My flesh shifted back into place. I touched it to make sure everything was how it should be. I'd never had issues with shifting back properly, but with Victor watching me, I couldn't help but become nervous that this would be the time I messed it up.

I lifted my head and looked around. "I haven't seen anything odd yet. Could I meet her? She might have seen something."

"You can talk to cats? Of course you can." Victor's smile was radiant. "How else would you communicate with Gertie? That's brilliant. She's just upstairs."

I followed Victor as he strode to the steps.

"Her name is Mariposa because of her unique facial markings. But he usually just called her Posey," he said.

"It sounds like you knew the owner well."

He faltered for a second before continuing up. "You could say that."

Victor led me to an office on the second floor. He inched the door open and slipped inside then held up a finger to let me know to wait. Behind the door, his voice murmured in reassuring notes.

After almost a minute, he ducked his head out. "She's ready for you. She's moody because I won't let her out of the office."

If anyone in this building deserved gentleness at the moment, it was the shop cat. I slipped into the small office next to Victor. With the desk in the middle and file cabinets lining the walls, it was barely big enough for the two of us. I gingerly moved a stack of old leather-bound books from the only chair in the room and sat down. Mariposa, a long-haired brown tabby, glowered at me from under the desk.

I relaxed my shoulders and lowered my hand until it hung limply between my knees. I blew out a swirl of magic toward her. Only witches could detect magic, so I was the only one who saw the petals as they floated to her face. A particularly large one landed on her nose and settled into her fur. Through the petals, I let my enchantment specialty work. I started with a twinge of curiosity and then built up the emotions, layer after layer of trust and relaxation but with curiosity slipped between each layer to encourage the cat to come out from hiding.

Mariposa was a beautiful cat. Her tabby markings almost looked like a monarch butterfly had landed on her face. She slunk out from the desk and sniffed at my hand before rubbing her petite body against my legs. She was more fluff than anything else. She weighed maybe six pounds, which was so small in comparison to Dani's cat, Charlie, who she'd stopped weighing when he crossed the thirty-pound threshold. To be fair, familiars were always extra large for their species. Gertie, my dairy-cow familiar, was almost as big as a Clydesdale horse.

I scratched the cat's head as she continued to rub against my legs, a loud purr vibrating through her body. I murmured the words to the spell that would let us communicate with one another. It wasn't so much a conversation as a transfer of mental images.

I closed my eyes and asked the first question. "Hi, sweet girl. Did you see what happened to the man who takes care of you?"

A flood of sensations went through me. Her paws batted at a closed door to a building as someone yelled from inside. She howled as things crashed out of sight.

"Oh no. Who let you out?" I continued to scratch her head.

More images entered my mind. The door was still closed. There was a feeling of hopelessness as she tapped at it, and then there were very large boots. They were black, with khaki pants over them. The image shifted as Mariposa was lifted from the ground and Harrison Abbott's face came into view. He was one of the local deputies.

"Did you hear or recognize any voices before that?"

The voice of Mariposa's owner filtered through, with a sense of contentment, as well as a woman's voice. The cat had been lying on the desk, half-asleep. It was hard to tell if the conversation was right before the incident or hours earlier.

I chewed on my lip. "When things were breaking, did you smell anything? Did you know who was downstairs?"

Something floral hit me. It was almost exactly like the scent I had encountered downstairs. I still couldn't tell if it was a perfume or a shampoo.

"Who smells like that?" I murmured.

Too many faces to count, both male and female, flitted through my mind. I sighed and released the connection. I continued to stroke her back for a few more seconds before standing and backing out of the room.

"Did she know anything helpful?" Victor asked, closing the door.

"She was locked in the room at the time and didn't see anything." I followed him downstairs. "I haven't noticed anything strange. Why do you think this should be on my desk?"

Victor ran his fingers through his hair, mussing it further. He sighed and leaned back against the wall. "Manual was a vampire."

"Oh… so you found fangs or something like that during the autopsy? Why didn't you start with that?"

He grimaced. "No. Vampires look like regular humans when they're dead. There wouldn't be anything strange about his physiology."

I blinked and cocked my head. Curiosity bubbled under the surface. "How did you know?"

He turned his head to me and held my gaze. His eyes were a brilliant blue. "Can you promise me something?"

"What?"

"If I tell you, you can't tell anyone else. Not Miranda. Not even your coven. This has to stay between us."

I balked at the idea of keeping information from my coven. Miranda, I didn't mind keeping secrets from. But Dani, Kim, and Heather? They knew me too well for that.

"For how long?"

Victor sagged and closed his eyes. "Never mind. I'll figure something else out."

I moved closer and squeezed his shoulder. "I'm in a coven with them because I trust them with my life."

"What about my life?"

I swallowed. "Your life too. Plus… though I wish I could

promise to keep secrets from them, Dani's one of the most powerful divination witches in the state. While I can hide things from Miranda all day long, Dani would take one look at my face and know I was hiding something from her in less than a minute."

"I know Dani can keep a secret. But can Kim?" he asked.

"Better than anyone."

"Okay. So… with the exception of your coven, and with the promise that you will get them to agree to the same, I'll tell you."

I held out my pinky.

He stared blankly at it.

I wiggled my pinky. "Blame Kim's kids. Lindsey likes to believe pinky promises are stronger than anything."

He linked his finger with mine and held my gaze. "I'm a vampire too."

I clamped my mouth shut, my face instinctively going blank to hide my shock. I kept secrets well from most people because I held my emotions close to my chest. "But I've seen you outside during the day."

Victor let out an unamused chuckle. "Vampires aren't like Dracula. That's a myth. But we're hardy. We're difficult to kill, because we usually heal so quickly. I don't know how a regular human could have done this."

"How quickly?"

"Very." He squeezed my hand. I hadn't noticed that he hadn't dropped my finger since making the promise. "Are you going to take the case or not?"

My mind whirled. *What else is a myth? Do vampires drink blood? Was Manual staked through the heart? Oh god. Victor might have just lost a friend, and he's relying on me to figure it out. I don't know anything.*

"I'll need to know more about vampires," I said.

Victor nodded. "We can read the section on vampires in the field guide together. I've never been the greatest teacher and would probably end up rambling about a random topic instead of telling you something useful."

"And I'll have to tell the city council something. I can't just claim a case without justification."

"You can tell them what he is. Just… keep how you know to yourself."

"Why are you hiding it?" I asked.

He looked away from me. "Most people think vampires are monsters. I haven't made it onto Miranda's list yet. And I'm not ready to have my friends look at me like I'm a bad guy."

I winced internally as I remembered reading the list of supernaturals in the field guide. *I told him vampire movies are my favorite horror films.* Tentatively, I wrapped my arm around his shoulder. I didn't know anything about vampires, but I knew Victor. And he was a gentle soul.

"Anyone who knows you won't think that."

"History would disagree." He relaxed into my hold. "But thank you."

"Your secret is safe with me." I gave him one last shoulder squeeze and stepped away. "I'll just have to be charming enough that they don't ask too many questions."

My words sounded more confident than I felt. I wasn't sure how I was going to convince the city council, but I would find a way.

# CHAPTER 3

I hefted the pail of chicken feed up as I stepped into the yard. Gertie peered at me from over the fence. I caught her eye. Taking a handful of seeds, I cleared my throat. I scattered the food around me. Chickens flocked to me, pecking at the ground as I moved through them.

"Well, you see, the victim was a vampire. So, um, it should be on my desk to triage." I winced. It didn't sound convincing to my ears. "Should I be using his name? Try to personalize it?"

Gertie grunted in agreement.

I set the pail down to reference my notes. After getting home the night before, I'd spent about an hour online, digging into the bookstore owner. Manual Delgado Perez had owned the place for over ten years. His online presence was minimal. The store had a page, and I found pictures of him in a few shots customers had uploaded but nothing from him or the store directly. I'd met him in passing a handful of times but couldn't have described him in any great detail. Looking at him now felt strange. There was a level of familiarity from buying books from him, but I didn't know him or anything about him on a personal level. I barely remembered his name.

Manual looked like he was in his mid to late forties. His dark-brown hair had a smattering of gray at the temples. In all the photos, he was dressed in a tweed jacket with patches on the elbows. Bronze, almost antique-looking cufflinks peeked out at the wrists. He gave off quintessential professor vibes. I could picture him as a background character in the beginning of an Indiana Jones movie, when Harrison Ford hadn't left for one of his adventures yet. And he was a vampire. And dead.

I shoved the phone into my pocket and shooed the chickens away from the bucket. Then I hoisted it back up and continued my circuit of the yard as a flock of almost thirty birds trailed after me.

"Okay. I should probably open with getting the call and then move on to Mr. Perez. Or Manual. Should I call him by his first name or his last?" I glanced over at Gertie.

Gertie stared back at me, her expression unamused. She'd never met any of the city council members, and even if she had, she doubted any of them would have taken her opinion seriously. Gertie had been disgruntled when I shared that councilman Edgar Graves accused me of looking unprofessional when I was seen riding on her back. She still wasn't pleased with my new role, which took me away from the farm more than she would like. So standing there, listening to me practice my speech, was very sweet of her.

"Doesn't using a person's name humanize them? And I should do that because I want them to care and give me the case. Or… is humanizing him the wrong thing? Should I be leaning into him being a vampire? But then they might think all vampires are monsters, and what if they find out about Victor?" I groaned. "Am I overthinking this? I should just go with Manual. Keep it simple, right?"

Gertie lowered her head to eat some grass.

"You're not being helpful."

She looked at me, maintaining eye contact, as she chewed.

"Fine. You are being helpful. Thank you for listening. So, we've decided I'll call him Manual."

I emptied out the last of the pail and moved on to the rest of my farm chores. Gertie followed diligently behind me, grunting or nestling her head against me at the right moments to give me feedback. After finishing up my portion of the chores, I led Gertie back to the barn. I brushed her out and allowed her to sneak a few pieces of apple from my pocket while I went through the latest iteration of my speech.

"Manual is super—no, preternatural. Preternatural. Why did they choose that word? Manual is preternatural. This case should be on my desk."

Gertie rested her head on my shoulder and exhaled into my hair. Through our familiar bond, I could feel the waves of reassurance she was sending my way. I scratched behind her ears and disentangled myself.

"Lindsey should be by in about an hour. Stay out of trouble until she gets here, okay?"

Gertie snorted and glowered at me as I strode out to my car. She had broken into the house the previous week to try to take a nap inside, where it was cooler, before Lindsey arrived. She had lain down on the couch, but it wasn't designed to hold an almost two-thousand-pound dairy cow. The couch had broken in half, and I was still grumpy at her for that.

Before I left, Gertie leaned into me with all her impossible weight, warm and solid. I rested my forehead against her side for just a second longer than necessary. No city council. No politics. Just us. And for a moment, the world felt manageable again.

As I drove into town, I practiced my arguments a few more times. I found a parking spot across the street from town hall and made my way inside. The receptionist glanced up as I walked through the door. She gave me her usual friendly smile and jerked her head back to indicate it was okay for me to head into the council meeting chambers. They met every Monday morning for a few hours and again throughout the week as the needs of the town dictated.

I let myself into the room and took a seat at the back. The council didn't have an audience that morning. The large room was mostly empty, with the city council sitting in a line at the back. Steven Bishop, the mayor, had a habit of standing during the meetings, which made them look like a cross between the last supper painting and a court room. He stood in a navy blue suit, with his jacket slung onto the chair behind me. The top button of his cream shirt was undone, and the sleeves of his shirt were rolled up to the elbows. His hair was clipped short with a light fade at the sides to keep it neat. Normally, he oozed approachability, but today he was pinching the bridge of his nose and sighing with exasperation.

My eyes tracked from him to the rest of the city council. Arthur was slouched in his seat, his legs stretched out in front of him and crossed at the ankles. He wore a tweed suit and a cream shirt. He was wiping his glasses, which he did whenever he needed to buy time to formulate an appropriate response. Every word out of his mouth was purposeful. Helen sat next to him. Despite the warm weather outside, she still had on a knit cardigan over a wrap dress. She held a massive crochet project in her lap and thrust the hook through the yarn, aggressively grabbing the next loop. On the other side of Steven were Edgar and Nicholas. Edgar, dressed in his usual suit, glowered at me and began fidgeting with his tie. He wasn't my biggest fan. Nicholas, compared to the rest, looked bored. He wore a Save the Whales T-shirt, board shorts, and sandals. He drummed his fingers on the table like he was counting down the minutes until the meeting was over. And seated at the end of the table was the newest addition to the city council, Amanda Yu, aka Mandy. She was in a gray skirt suit. Her black hair was pulled into a severe pony tail. She didn't strike me as relaxed enough to go by Mandy, but the first time I met her, she'd insisted on it as she vigorously shook my hand.

Mandy's calm, even voice filled the room. "I don't mean to throw a wrench in things, but it is technically a state park. Fireworks are banned there, so we should find an alternate location to set them off."

Arthur slipped his glasses back on. "We've been using that spot for over twenty years. I don't understand why it needs to change now."

"Just because we've allowed people to break the law in the past doesn't mean we should continue to do so now," Mandy responded.

My eyes glazed over as they continued to bicker about where they would be launching the town's fireworks display. With the Fourth of July just over two weeks away, I was surprised they hadn't ironed that out already.

Steven flopped down into his seat. "Let's table that for this afternoon. We have someone waiting patiently to speak with us, and I have a feeling this conversation is going to take longer than any of us would like."

All eyes turned to me. I stood and held my head high as I crossed the room to the banister separating the city council chambers table from the rows of benches where people would sit in during open sessions.

"Did you have business for us?" Steven had a pleading look in his eyes. Apparently, the fireworks argument had been going on for a long time.

"Yes. I… the murder of Mr. Manual Delgado Perez should be on my desk." I held my gaze steady on Steven's face.

He was the friendliest of the bunch and seemed to trust me the most. Helen was a different story. I had a feeling that if I looked into her eyes too long, she would pick up on one of my half-truths. After being a school teacher for most of her life, she had a sense for it.

"Victor called me out to take a look at the scene. He had some concerns over the level of violence," I said.

"And…? What did you find?" Edgar asked.

My gaze flicked to his. His usual glower in my presence was still in place. The door opened behind me. I glanced back as Miranda let herself into the room.

"Well?" Edgar barked.

"Manual is—was—a vampire."

"Huh?" Mandy sat forward. "I don't recall seeing any vampires on the list. Are you sure?"

"They have a tendency not to self-identify." Miranda came up next to me. "They're a private group but mostly harmless."

Nicholas straightened in his seat and smiled. "How many are there? What are they like?"

"We're getting off topic," Arthur said. "I believe Miss Miller was making an argument that the case should be on her desk. If Mr. Delgado was not on a list, how can you be sure of his affiliations?"

"It's not an exact science, but there is magic available that can help me identify a preternatural individual."

"And you cast this spell?" Mandy asked.

I opened my mouth to respond, but Arthur cut me off. "We gave her this position because she's the expert. Does this really need a lengthy discussion? I move to have the case transferred to her desk."

"Seconded," Helen said.

"Of course you would second it." Edgar shifted in his seat, his scowl deepening. "I, for one, think if they haven't gone through the trouble of informing us of their presence, they shouldn't fall under *her* purview."

Nicholas scoffed. "It's taxpayer dollars either way. I wouldn't call it special treatment."

"Is it more or less taxpayer money for Miss Miller to be involved?" Mandy asked.

Arthur sighed and took off his glasses to clean.

Helen rolled her eyes and continued to crochet. "It depends on if the investigation would require the sheriff's department to work overtime. At the end of the day, it's honestly probably a wash since, if Megan is right and Mr. Perez was a vampire, Chris would need to pull her in anyway. Can we vote already? The motion is already on the floor, and I would like to spend some time today with my grandkids."

Steven went down the line, taking the vote. It was no surprise that Arthur, Helen, and Nicholas were all yeses, while Edgar was an emphatic no.

Mandy leaned forward to give her vote. "Yes, but with a caveat. I don't know you yet, so to get my support in the future, I'll expect an update by the end of the week."

"I can agree with that addendum," Nicholas said.

Helen grumbled.

Nicholas shot her a wide smile. "What? It will at least make the Friday meeting more interesting."

Helen packed up her yarn. "I was hoping we wouldn't have a Friday meeting."

"This close to the Fourth? Not a chance," Nicholas said.

I nodded to them and backed away from the banister. I had less than five days to make progress on this investigation, so I needed to get out there to begin the interviews. I texted Victor on my way out.

I got the case.

> **VICTOR:**
> Excellent. I'm working on the autopsy now. Why don't you come by for dinner, and we can have that talk I promised.

I look forward to it.

Miranda trailed after me. "I didn't think you had it in you."

I stiffened and came to a stop. "Have what in me?"

"The nerve to take a case away from the sheriff without so much as a conversation first." Miranda paused next to me. "Should I be proud?"

My stomach clenched, and I shoved my phone into my pocket. I'd been so focused on my presentation that I'd forgotten to call Chris. *Is he going to be mad? Shoot. I should have talked to him first. He probably would have backed me, and I wouldn't have had to get into it with Edgar like that.*

"I'm also surprised your spell worked." Miranda stepped in front of me and studied my face. "The only spells I know of only work on living creatures."

"I didn't know identification magic was your specialty."

Miranda narrowed her eyes. Her magic was more similar to Kim's than mine or Dani's. She specialized in abjuration magic, which primarily dealt with protecting people or places. "It's not. But that doesn't mean I'm not knowledgeable."

I gave her a professional smile and deflected. "My coven's always been good at looking into the past." I stepped around her. "Now, if you'll excuse me, I've got an investigation to run."

"Good luck!" Miranda called after me. "I'm looking forward to hearing your update to the council."

I strode out of the building, my shoulders rolled back to make myself look confident. Instead of just solving the murder for Victor, I also needed to do it for Miranda and the newest councilwoman, Mandy. I hated having people looking over my shoulder while I worked, but I had to identify the killer quickly, before they figured out I hadn't been entirely truthful in there—and hopefully not alienate Chris in the process. I had five days to not fall flat on my face.

# CHAPTER 4

I pulled to a stop in front of the sheriff's station, which was housed in a historical three-story brick building downtown. Every inch of the interior had been remodeled just over a year ago. While city hall was still stately, it had a worn-around-the-edges look when I really inspected it closely. The sheriff's station had none of that. The hardwood floors gleamed, and the exposed brick walls in the foyer gave the place an almost homey character. It had become one of my favorite buildings in town.

I walked toward the desk for the office manager, Peggy Wright. She had worked for the station for as long as I could remember and had looked like she was in her forties for the entire time. Before going in, I'd applied a green eye shadow that was spelled to reveal people's supernatural auras to me. Peggy was just back from her honeymoon, and I half expected to see something unusual about her when I approached. But she had the same big hair, bifocal glasses, and high-waisted pantsuit she always wore, with not a single odd thing about her aura. She was a standard human. For the life of me, I couldn't figure out how she'd managed to look forty for over twenty years.

Peggy smiled as I came to a stop in front of her desk. "Megan! I didn't know you were coming in today. What can I help you with?"

"Is Chris in?"

Peggy nodded. "I'll page him to see if he's free."

As she typed out a message on her computer, I took a step back and sat in the chairs lining the walls. They reminded me of chairs you'd find in a doctor's office—dark brown, with a leather look except they felt plasticky under my fingers. They were designed to be comfortable for long waits but easy to clean because, as with a doctor's office, you never knew what might be spilled on them.

I crossed my legs and folded my hands over my knee, holding my posture rigid in the chair. Peggy and I had interacted regularly for the last two months, and she had always been sweet to me. I wasn't sure if it was because she was particularly susceptible to my enchantment magic or for another reason. Most people, when they were within about ten feet of me, found me likable and wanted to help. She had seemed really happy overall, though, so I liked to think it wasn't the magic but her engagement, and recent marriage, to Robert Wright, the former sheriff. After his retirement, I was surprised to see her still working at the station. They had been two peas in a pod for years. But she struck me as someone who needed to stay busy, like me, and the retired life probably wasn't hectic enough for her.

"He's ready for you," Peggy said.

I stood and made my way back to Chris's office. He could have claimed any room in the three-story building, but he had taken a small one on the first floor because he liked to be in the thick of things. His door was already open as I approached. I rapped my knuckles against the doorframe and entered.

The office was tidy but homey. Chris had a few framed photos on his desk as well as a large earthenware coffee mug.

I recognized the faint scent of Heather's signature honey-roasted coffee, and my stomach gave an appreciative rumble. I smiled. She made the best coffee in town. I focused on the scent and the steady hum of the building around me. Solid walls. Familiar faces. Safe ground.

Chris beamed at me as he cleared a few files off his desk. "Hey, Megan. What can I do for you today?"

I perched at the edge of the chair across from him. My palms were sweaty. I curled my fingers around my knees. "I wanted to talk to you about Mr. Delgado's case."

"Oh?" He leaned back. "Did you find something last night?"

I nodded. "City council tasked me with looking into it."

He grabbed the folder of incident-report forms I had filled out over the past month and flipped through it. "Did I miss the form?"

"I—"

Miranda's words played in my head. I hadn't meant to take the case away from him without having a conversation first. *I'm not good at this. I should be better at being on a team by now.*

"I'm sorry. I got ahead of myself. It's my second case, and I skipped ahead to reporting it to city council."

Chris nodded and dropped the file. "Don't worry about it."

I studied him. There had been a flash of emotion in his eyes. *Did I hurt him, or is it actually okay?* The only feelings my mother had trained me to pick up on, from a young age, were the aggressive ones like anger or hatred. For someone who was skilled at affecting people's emotions, I was terrible at picking up on them.

"We weren't too far into the investigation yet. We had identified two persons of interest we planned on tracking down today." Chris lifted another folder from his desk and flipped it open. "Do you need their info, or have you already zeroed in on a lead?"

"That would be great." I flushed. "Honestly, I don't have much yet. All I know so far is that the victim was a vampire. I don't really know much yet."

Chris froze and looked up at me. "A vampire, huh?"

I nodded.

He shook his head and began jotting names down on a Post-it note. "I guess I shouldn't be surprised they're real. I swear, I'm getting to the point where you could come tell me there was a yeti in the waiting room, and my first thought would be *Does she mean the cooler brand or the abominable snowman?*"

I smiled. Since discovering witches were real, he had been thrown into the deep end. But he rolled with the punches better than most. "So, where are you guys at with your investigation?"

"We're pretty much at the same place. We haven't delved into it much yet. The only two people he seemed to have frequent disagreements with were Douglas Howard and Tiffany Malone."

I grabbed the Post-it from him and stared at the names. Under Douglas's name were the words *Glass & Shadow Collectibles,* and next to Tiffany's name, Chris had written *Parents for Responsible Reading.*

"Who are these guys?" I asked.

Chris capped his pen. "Douglas runs an antiquities shop. He and Manual were frequently trying to acquire the same books, and from what we've heard, it could get heated on occasion. Last month, we responded to a complaint at a local auction, and Bruno—Douglas's bodyguard—and Manual came to blows over a map collection. And Tiffany Malone is a very vocal concerned parent. I would be surprised if you haven't seen her at one of the council meetings yet. She's there almost every week, petitioning to have books banned from the local library. She also pressures local bookstores to stop carrying them, and Manual refused to do so. Instead, he started a banned-books display."

I tried to smother a laugh, but it came out as a strangled snort. Books had been my refuge for most of my adult life, and I suspected I was a bit like Manual. Whenever someone told me I couldn't read something, it just made me want to read it even more.

"We were trying to figure out if he had any family in the area but came up blank." Chris chuckled and shook his head as tapped his fingers against the desk. "Vampire, though. Shoot. I wonder how much time we would have wasted before we figured out something about him was off."

"Thanks for the leads." I stood. "I should get started on this. Mandy is expecting a case update by the end of the week."

"Is she giving you trouble?"

I shrugged. "Too soon to tell."

He followed me to the door. "I'll keep my fingers crossed that she turns out to be more like Helen and less like Edgar."

I gave him a one-armed hug then stepped into the hall. Chris walked me out. There was still a stiffness in his shoulders, but he was chatting amiably with me about lunch plans later in the week. I studied him out of the corner of my eye. He was one of the nicest guys I knew and a total marshmallow when he was around his wife. I still couldn't tell if he was upset I hadn't looped him in before talking to the city council. There were moments when he almost seemed relieved. Even if he was angry, I doubted he would bring it up.

We fell into a companionable, but tense, silence as we stepped into the lobby. Thanking him again, I turned toward and approached the front door, only to walk directly into Harrison's back. I stumbled away, mumbling an apology as he reached out to steady me.

Harrison was tall, with an impressive arm span. In another life, he could have been a competitive swimmer. He held my shoulder with one hand, and the other was pressed to the back of a disorientated-looking teenage boy. Between the three of us, we covered almost half the lobby, with Harrison stretched out like Laffy Taffy. The boy peeked at me through a curtain of teal hair. He had the look of a drowned rat, his hair and clothes plastered to his slender frame. It took a second for it to register that the slight sheen on his skin wasn't water. A very subtle glow pulsed around him.

"Sorry, ma'am." Harrison patted my arm. "Didn't see you there."

My eyes flicked between the boy and Harrison. The only reason he would glow like that was that he was a supernatural entity like me. But it wasn't a glow I recognized. I hadn't encountered whatever he was before.

"No worries. Is everything all right here?" I asked.

"Yep. We're all good. Ethan, here, seems to have had a rough night. Just trying to get him someplace warm until his sister can come pick him up." Harrison patted Ethan on the back.

My eyes flicked between Harrison, Ethan, Chris, and Peggy, who was typing away at her keyboard behind her desk. *Just because he's not a regular human doesn't mean this is my business. I've already got a case. But... what does Harrison mean by a rough night? Do I need to fill out an incident report form on this?*

"Mind if I chat with him for a second?"

Harrison quirked his eyebrow.

I gave him a professional smile. "I've had my fair share of rough nights."

Harrison shrugged and stepped off to the side.

I inched toward Ethan. He didn't push the hair out of his face as he followed me with his eyes.

I lowered my voice. “Are you all right, kid?”

“I—do I know you?”

I shook my head. “I work for the city council. I’m… a consultant of sorts.”

He fiddled with the sleeves of his long-sleeved T-shirt. It had the name of a band I didn’t recognize on the front, and the sleeves were long, half covering his hands. His nails were painted black.

“It’s my job to report to them on incidents involving… special people.” I tried to give him a reassuring smile.

He shuffled a step back. “There’s nothing special about me.”

I took a seat near him and relaxed my body to try and give off a nonthreatening vibe. “I don’t know about that. You look pretty cool to me.”

He eased himself into a seat next to me and continued to peer at me through his hair. “Are you, like, a social worker or something? My home life is good. I promise. I don’t usually find myself wandering around downtown like that.”

“Like what?”

“Confused.” He leaned toward me, some of the tension leaving his body as he became accustomed to my calming aura. “I don’t know how I got there.”

“What—”

The front doors slammed open, and a girl with dusty-rose-colored hair stomped into the room. She had the same slender build and wide expressive eyes as Ethan. While his were confused, hers were filled with rage. She wore a pair of scuffed Dr. Martens, cutoff shorts, and an off-the-shoulder T-shirt with the same band name as Ethan’s plastered across the chest. She glowered at me and spun toward Harrison.

“Is he being detained?” she snarled.

Harrison held his hands up. “You must be Rowan.”

“I asked a question.” She held her head up, her chin jutting forward. “Is he free to go?”

"Um. Yes?" Harrison glanced behind her at me.

"I—" I shook my head and stood up.

Rowan spun on her heel and thrust her hand toward her brother. "Ethan. We're leaving."

He levered himself up and shuffled after her, his head hanging low. I stood there, watching him leave. He wasn't being detained. He'd committed no crime as far as I knew, so there wasn't a form for me to complete. But he seemed so confused.

*Should I follow them?* I glanced down at the Post-it note in my hand, with two names on it. I folded it and slid it into my pocket. While I wasn't sure if Ethan needed my help, I knew Manual had been murdered. I had to focus on the investigation.

Douglas was the first name on the list. As I strode to my truck, I pulled up his business page on my phone. Glass and Shadow had been in business for five years and had a storefront in downtown Oak Harbor. Almost everything on Douglas's personal page was private, so all I had to go on was a single photo of a man in his forties, wearing a tailored charcoal suit. He had sharp, angular features and eyes that stared intently at the camera. It was only one photo, but he gave the impression he was a man who knew exactly what he wanted and expected to get it.

# CHAPTER 5

It took almost an hour to get to Oak Harbor from Point Pleasant. The route was mostly empty that time of day and wound through tree-lined streets, allowing my mind to wander. With so little to go on, I wasn't sure what to expect when I arrived. I had spent most of my life on a farm and avoided going into town as much as I could. Growing up as part of the infamous Miller family had been rough, and it had only been about ten months since our name had been cleared. While no one batted an eye when they met me or heard my name, old habits of keeping to myself died hard. There was still that voice in the back of my mind that asked when things were going to change again—when I would lose all my friends. It was hard to shake, so I still ordered most things online and went through intermediaries to sell my produce and eggs at the local farmers markets. I had never in my life set foot into a fancy business like Glass and Shadow.

My hands were sweaty as I parked. I'd tried to rehearse my questions on the ride up but, without knowing what to expect, had floundered when I got past hello. *No time like the present.* I pulled a notebook from my backpack and jotted down a few ideas. I wasn't the best at creating lists.

My thoughts scattered, because if he answered one way, the questions that followed would be different. I tried to mind map it out. I circled my main questions and then drew lines to potential follow-up questions. It has hard to know what directions they would go, though, because I didn't know anything about who Douglas was or what he did. The website for his business had been sparse and more atmospheric than informative, as if people who went to him were expected to already know what he was about. It felt like I was jumping into the deep end instead of wading into the shallows.

I circled my primary questions one more time.

*Who is Douglas, and what does he do?*
*What was his altercation with Manual about?*

From those two base questions, the unknowns spiraled out. As much as I tried to prep, I would have to figure out my follow-up questions on the fly. I stowed my notebook, climbed out of my truck, and made my way over to the storefront.

Glass and Shadow wasn't hard to find. The two-story building had a front that was glass all the way from the ground to the sharply sloping roof. The glass was clear, but because of how the walls were shaped, I could only see a few feet inside before it became gloomy.

I straightened to my full height and strode into the building. It took a second for my eyes to adjust. The interior was even more peculiar looking than the exterior. The first half of the room was warm and inviting, with sunlight streaming through the windows. There were comfortable-looking couches facing the windows, and the whole place smelled of cedar and books. Behind the couches, the ceiling came down at an angle and then sloped upward, creating an odd, almost V shape in the center that cut the light in the room in half.

The front of the store was bright and airy, while the back was warm but dimly lit. I stepped into the darkened half. The walls were lined with glass enclosures, and wooden tables bisected the room. The place was bright enough to read by, but the lighting seemed perfectly calibrated to prevent any harm to old paper.

Douglas emerged from the shadows. "Are you looking for something in particular?" His voice was like liquid honey. There was an intensity in his gaze as he sidled up next to me. "Or are you just browsing?"

"I—what is it that you do here?" I asked.

"I put people together. People who want something…" He gestured toward me and then at the glass cases. "And people who have it. Although my specialty is finding a person who has books or other written documentation."

I nodded along and studied him as he spoke, looking for any sign that he was supernatural. His hair was slicked back, his widow's peak pronounced, and his angular face led to deep shadows under his cheekbones. But nothing in the air around him indicated he was anything other than a normal man.

"I heard you had a recent argument with Manual over a book you were trying to purchase."

He lifted his right shoulder and spread out his hands, and a predatory smile crossed his face. "Friendly banter between two similarly motivated people in the same field."

"Were you trying to buy the book for a specific customer?"

He cocked his eyebrow and snapped his fingers. The shadows behind him moved, and a giant of a man lumbered forward. He was as tall as Harrison but so much broader. His suit jacket clung to his bulging muscles. He glowered at me, his eyes glittering under his pronounced brow. He stepped between me and Douglas and shoved a white business card toward me. It was tiny compared to his massive hand. My gaze flicked between him, the card, and Douglas, who was standing at ease behind him, inspecting his fingernails.

I reached forward and took the card. "What's this for?"

"I am tired—no, *exhausted,* weary, at my wits' end. I cannot, and will not, deal with that man's constant complaints and allegations. If he has something to say, he can say it to my attorney," Douglas said.

I stared at him, wishing yet again that I was as good at reading people as Dani was. "That would be hard for him to do."

Douglas dropped his hand and sighed. "What is it this time?"

"Manual is dead."

In the space of maybe half a second, his expression shifted from bored to something else and then back to bored. It happened too fast for me to tell whether he was surprised.

He crossed his hands in front of him and pursed his lips. "Bruno? Please add a reminder to my calendar about sending flowers to Mr. Perez's estate."

The large man in front of me grunted and reached into his jacket to extract a cell phone. As he did so, something shifted under his arm. I blinked as it registered. A small white dog, cradled in what looked like a baby sling, poked its head out and yawned. Bruno pecked at the screen of his phone with his meaty fingers before sliding it back into his pocket. His hand slid over the head of the dog, scratching it behind its ears, before he closed his suit jacket again, hiding both the dog and his phone.

*What on earth? He's... he's wearing a dog. Why is he wearing a dog?* Whether it was a young puppy or a teacup Pomeranian was hard to tell in the few seconds the dog had been visible. I blinked again, trying to remember my next question.

"Was that all, Miss...?" Douglas stretched out the word *Miss* until it was more like a long *s* sound than anything else.

"Miller." I held my hand out to shake. He stared at it, and I let my hand drop between us. "Megan Miller. I'm looking into Manual's death. Since you… are similarly motivated individuals in the same field, I wondered if you knew anyone who might have had issues with Mr. Perez."

Bruno stepped to the side, blocking Douglas from my view. He crossed his arms, careful not to crowd the dog hidden in his jacket, and scowled down at me. The combination of his body language, shaved head, dark-brown eyes, and furrowed brow told me that no further questions would be tolerated. I had a feeling if I said anything other than "Have a nice day," Bruno would escort me from the building.

I fished around in my own pocket, pulled out a business card the city council had been kind enough to produce for me, and handed it over. "If you think of anything or… see anything weird that might be connected, call me."

Bruno took the card and jerked his head toward the door. I held my hands out at my sides and stepped back. He cracked his knuckles and crossed his arms, his suit pulling tight around his massive biceps. I stepped back, forcing a professional smile onto my face. I didn't take my eyes off him until I'd reached the couches.

"Thank you for your time." I turned on my heel and strode from the building, my head held high and shoulders back. I walked to my truck, doing my best to exude confidence, until I was safe behind my wheel.

Once inside the truck, I exhaled sharply and slid down my seat. That whole interaction had been strange. Douglas wasn't part of the supernatural community, but Bruno scared me almost as much as facing down a werewolf. They were hiding something. But that didn't mean they were involved. Unfortunately, it seemed their emotions around Manual were too negative for my charming aura to have made an impact. I slid my notebook out of my bag and looked at my two core questions. The first one—*Who is Douglas and what does he do?*—had only been half answered. And the second—

*What was the altercation with Manual about?*—was still a giant question mark.

*Am I moving too slowly?*

I continued to stare at the questions. They were similar to the core questions I had for Tiffany—who she was, why her disagreements with Manual were worse than those with other bookstore owners in the area, and whether she was a violent person. *What if I don't find anything useful out with her either? Will I have wasted the day?*

My chest constricted. I focused on my breathing, which had sped up while I was staring at the page. *I can't have a panic attack right now. I don't have time for this.* My breath quickened again, and I stopped and held it until my eyes burned. I breathed out thoroughly, emptying my lungs, before taking another breath.

*Not everything is going to be as easy as running a farm. I can do this.*

I packed up my bag and headed back to Point Pleasant. I had one more person to interview and then my dinner with Victor. Hopefully, I would learn something helpful in the next two stops. I didn't like the idea of going back to Oak Harbor to interview Douglas a second time. If only future investigations included fewer shadowy men and more French fries.

# CHAPTER 6

Tiffany posted her entire life online. After twenty minutes of scrolling through her page, I was pretty sure I knew everything she had eaten that week, what she really thought about the latest Marvel movie, and where she went on a daily basis. The night of Manual's murder, she had posted about heading to a PTA meeting, and then her activities had picked back up at breakfast. There was an unusual gap in her amount of activity. That was the only day of the week she didn't talk about what she'd eaten for dinner.

I pulled to a stop outside the middle school and crossed the street to the baseball field across the way. Tiffany must have been in the running for most involved parent of the year, because based on her social media posts, she lived and breathed school spirit. She was part of the PTA, a frequent school chaperone, and a volunteer for pretty much every position imaginable, from crossing guard to assistant baseball coach. I almost felt bad for her son. There probably wasn't an hour out of the day when she didn't have eyes on him. If she were a cool mom, he probably wouldn't mind, but based on the intense look in her eyes and the tight-lipped smile her son adopted in all his photos, I doubted it.

I stopped at the end of the small set of bleachers and watched. Tiffany was easy to spot. She wasn't much taller than the kids, but she had a well-practiced poise. Her blonde hair was swept up into a high ponytail, and she wore a pair of white pants and a polo shirt with the school's logo emblazoned across the back. Even from a distance, I could tell she wasn't wearing her normal jewelry. In almost every photo, she wore pearls. She probably had a carrying case for them for events like this.

While I stood there watching, the kids dropped down to the ground with their legs kicked out in front of them and watched as the coach and Tiffany strode onto the field. I was too far away to hear what he was saying, and his baritone voice was muffled by the wind. Tiffany grabbed a bat and took up a position at the batter's box while the coach walked out to the pitcher's mound. They demonstrated hand positioning before he sent a fast ball hurtling toward Tiffany. A loud crack filled the air as Tiffany's bat made contact with the ball, which flew past the stands faster than my eye could track. Tiffany lowered the bat and did a small curtsy to the sound of kids hooting and hollering their praise.

After that demonstration, the kids lined up to take their turns in the box, and Tiffany wandered over to the benches. She picked up a pink water bottle with her name on the side in rhinestones. I studied her for a few more seconds as she stood there, shouting out encouragement to the kids between sips of water.

I made my way over to her. I'd reapplied the green eyeshadow that I had spelled to help me identify supernatural beings. Other than her glittery name on the water bottle, there was nothing shiny about Tiffany. Her makeup was matte and understated. There was no supernatural shimmer or haze in the air around her. As I got closer, she glanced over at me. Her eyes narrowed for a split second before she plastered a friendly smile on her face, revealing perfectly straight white teeth.

"Can I help you?" Tiffany stepped between me and the field. "I don't think I've seen you around before. Are you related to one of the kids?"

I moved closer until she was within ten feet of me. With my specialization in enchantment magic, people who were in close proximity to me tended to give me the benefit of the doubt. "I'm actually here to see you. Tiffany Malone, right? You're the head of Parents for Responsible Reading, aren't you?"

"That's me." Her body language shifted. She was somehow both taller, like she was proud, and more fragile. She folded her hands in front of her, her lips pressed into a thin smile, and a furrow formed in her brow. "As a concerned parent, I just want to make sure the community is safe for my kids. Not only physically but emotionally and intellectually as well. Shouldn't all parents care about what their children are consuming?"

She almost sounded reasonable. If I hadn't read through her list of objectionable books before coming, I might have been nodding along. But Tiffany took issue with whole genres. She seemed to despise all things magic because she felt they were a slippery slope to children making deals with the devil. It was easier to ask what was on her approved list than what she wanted out of schools, libraries, and bookstores.

"I heard you've been having some issues getting local businesses to agree," I said.

Tiffany lowered her head and then peered up at me through her eyelashes. "Some are more concerned with profits than with child safety. It's disheartening."

"Is that what Manual said?" I asked.

She shook her head, her eyes taking on a fierce gleam.

"That man. He said he wasn't about to start letting *some woman* dictate to him what he could or could not sell in his place of business."

"Wow."

My mind sifted through the questions I had written down in the truck. She seemed willing to talk about Manual, but I didn't want to spook her too early and lose my chance to dive into the more important questions. *Or should I just start with the tough ones?* I focused on my breathing, working to keep any sign of my nerves from showing. She was a shark, and I would have to tread lightly if I wanted this conversation to be productive.

"Sounds like he was difficult to deal with. So he gave you a lot of grief over your mission?"

"He's impossible." She flung her arms up. "I would make a few reasonable requests, and his response was to start a section of the store that featured the very books I was trying to protect our children from. Whenever I would add a new one to the list online, it would go up the next day at his store. Sometimes on sale even. Can you believe it? Honestly, I can't wait until his store goes out of business. The other mothers in my group agree. His place needs to be boycotted."

"That's probably not necessary," I said.

She pursed her lips, her eyes narrowing. She crossed her arms. "Oh? You think concerned parents should just let this stand?"

"No… I… it's just with Manual's death, who knows if the store will even stay open?"

She blinked and lowered her arms. "Dead?"

I nodded. "Yesterday."

"I am not one to speak ill of the dead. I'll pray for him." Her eyes flicked toward the kids practicing their baseball swings. "Lord knows he probably needs it."

The last of the kids stepped up to bat. Tiffany inched

backward and jerked her head toward him. "I should probably head back over. It was nice meeting you, Miss…?"

"Miller. Name's Megan." I held my hand out to her. "I actually just had one more question for you if you have another minute."

She shook my hand. "Another question?"

"Where were you last night?" I continued to shake her hand and maintained eye contact.

"Are you a cop or something?"

"Or something." I gave her a professional smile and continued to hold her gaze. "Can you tell me where you were last night?"

"At the school. I was doing volunteer work for the PTA. Almost all the other mothers flaked, so it was on me and Miss Allen to make all the signs for the local bake sale. I'm so glad Reggie's dad wasn't working late last night and could watch him. I didn't get home until after two in the morning. Is that all?"

I nodded and watched as she sauntered back to the coach. Tiffany clearly didn't like Manual very much, but she'd seemed surprised to hear about his death. Although the entire conversation had felt more like a performance than a genuine exchange. *Plus, who makes bake sale signs until two in the morning?*

I returned to my truck and climbed inside then drove a few blocks away and found a quiet spot to sit and think. Two suspects, both clearly human. Douglas was higher on my list than Tiffany, though I wasn't clearing either one. But I also hadn't conclusively found anything.

*Is Edgar right? How am I supposed to keep this on my desk? He'll want to take it away if I don't have something by the end of the week. If my only leads are human, then it would go to Chris. And Victor…*

*Stop it.* I pushed the negative thoughts to the back of my

mind and went back through my to-do list for the day. I had interviewed both suspects. Now all that was left to do was to meet up with Victor and learn more about vampires. He had been so certain a human couldn't have killed Manual, and I needed to understand why.

# CHAPTER 7

Victor lived in a two-story Craftsman house with a single-story extension on the back that housed the town's morgue. It would have looked like a standard home if it weren't for the strange-looking extra chimneys for the crematorium in the back. The entire first floor was dedicated to the funeral home and Victor's role as medical examiner. Everything on that floor was in soft, inviting shades of beige that always put me at ease.

I took the stairs up to his private quarters, where the paint scheme shifted to darker colors. I hovered on the landing. He knew I was coming, but I still felt like an intruder entering his personal space. I knocked on the door.

"Come on in!" Victor shouted through the door, his voice muffled. "I'm in the kitchen."

I swallowed and forced my hands to unclench. Whenever I was nervous, I tended to tense up. Too much of my life had been spent resisting my fight-or-flight instincts. My enchantment magic hadn't always given me the aura of likability. From the age of eighteen—when my magic came in—until ten months ago, the response I'd gotten from people had been the exact opposite. People had distrusted me on sight. Fighting reinforced their opinions of me and always made things worse. And running just triggered that part of people's minds that saw me as prey. It was better to stand tall, look confident, and bluff my way through situations. I wasn't sure if I would ever get used to the change. Being liked felt foreign, and part of me was still waiting for the other shoe to drop.

"You've got this. It's just dinner. A professional dinner. You're here to learn," I murmured. My shoulders relaxed, and I pushed the door inward.

I had only been inside Victor's apartment upstairs once before. It had a logical layout. There was the delicious scent of bacon filling the air. I followed the scent to the kitchen and paused in the archway.

Victor stood with his back to me. He wore his standard Regency-era suit, except he'd taken off the tailcoat, which hung over the back of a chair at the kitchen island. The sleeves of his white shirt were rolled up and pinned above his elbows while he cooked. His hair was in its usual pristine pompadour, and he must have recently trimmed his beard because it seemed shorter than usual. I studied him as he cooked. His choice of clothes had always seemed like a fun eccentricity.

*How old is he?* I didn't know anything about vampires outside of what I'd learned from movies and books.

"I hope you like carbonara." Victor drained water from the pasta and cracked an egg. "I probably should have asked. But I remembered you eating the pork chops at Dani's wedding, and I always see you with milkshakes at Slice of Life, so I assumed there wouldn't be any dietary restrictions there."

I claimed a seat at the island. "It smells amazing."

Victor shot me a relieved smile over his shoulder then returned to prepping the food.

I put my hands on the counter and held myself perfectly

still on the stool. My gaze bounced around the room, taking in the small details. Victor had an impressive collection of cast-iron kitchenware hanging on the back wall. His appliances were new, and the stovetop used gas. There was a vase of white lilies on the counter, and sitting at the edge of the island was the *Pacific Northwest Paranormal Field Guide,* by Harriet Spellman. Its green cover stood out against the white marble, its chipped golden foil almost matching the gold veins running through the counter.

Victor hummed as he continued to cook. He moved around the kitchen smoothly and confidently. He sprinkled parmesan into the pan and then grabbed tongs to mix the ingredients.

"How are you holding up?" I asked.

Victor shrugged. "Manual and I weren't very close. I would pet sit for him on occasion. And he special ordered books for me a few times."

"Huh." My eyes darted back to the field guide. "I assumed you knew him better."

Victor pulled a loaf of garlic bread from the oven and placed it on a wire rack to cool. "Because I wanted the case on your desk?"

"Yeah, you seemed… stressed about it."

"I was." He bent to retrieve a bottle of wine from under the counter. He held it up, showing me that it was a pinot grigio, and smiled. "Want a glass with dinner?"

"Sure." My heart skipped a beat. I pulled my hands into my lap to hide my clenching fists. *Stop being so nervous. It's dinner. A professional dinner. He smiles at everyone. I need to refocus on why I'm here.* "Why were you stressed about it?"

He set down two wineglasses and popped the cork to the bottle. "It's complicated. Some of it's in the guide, but not everything. Why don't you read it first, and then we can talk?"

I grabbed the book and flipped through the pages until I

reached the section on vampires. The first thing I noticed was an illustration of a man in a suit. There was nothing special about him. He looked completely normal. I glanced up at Victor. He wasn't looking at me. Instead, he was focused on cutting the bread and plating the food.

I ducked my head and began to read. I wasn't the fastest reader, so I skimmed the sections, trying to pull out important details. I paused when I reached the section on feeding.

> The most common misconception is that vampires consume blood. This myth can be directly traced to a single vampire, Vlad the Impaler. However, it is noteworthy that Vlad's obsession with blood manifested prior to his creation, so it does not appear that it had any connection to his status as a vampire. There have been numerous vampires since then who have been inspired by his notoriety, but most of the vampires I interviewed appeared to be embarrassed by the connection.

I let out a breath and continued reading. While the section was only a few pages long, it was jam-packed with information. Vampires were created by other vampires. They were believed to be immortal and became more powerful and harder to kill with age. The older they were, the quicker they healed. With very old vampires, healing was almost instantaneous. The largest section, by far, was on their feeding habits. Instead of consuming blood, they ate emotions, almost like plants consumed sunlight. They needed to surround themselves with it. They were also, unsurprisingly, secretive, and most of what was known about their society was based on conjecture, with the most popular theory being that a vampire Council of Kings ruled over the entire world. Unlike the dryad entry, the suggested-reading section listed a single book—although the author noted it might be difficult to find as it had been out of print since 1782.

I tapped the page. "So, it says here that the older a vampire is, the harder they are to kill. You said it would have taken a lot to kill Manual. I'm assuming he was old. Do you know when he was created?"

"I'm not sure of the exact year. He said sometime in the mid-1400s." Victor slid a plate of pasta toward me. "The rumor was he came over in one of the early Spanish colonies."

"Is that considered old by vampire standards?"

Victor took a bite of his carbonara and chewed it slowly. "It's subjective. He was older than most but by no means one of the oldest in the region. He was old enough that he would have been very difficult to kill. At least for a normal human."

"What if they used a weapon, like a bat?" I asked.

"Possibly. We heal so quickly around wounds that figuring out what killed him has been difficult."

"So, old enough to be hard to kill. The weapon might have been a bat." I took a bit of the food. Flavor exploded in my mouth. The pasta was perfectly creamy, with a nice savory flavor from the pancetta. It was perfect. "This is really good. Where did you learn how to cook like this?"

"I lived in New York for a while."

"How long were you there?"

"About fifty years," he said.

My eyes widened, and I almost dropped the fork. "And you've been here for at least twenty. How old are you?"

Victor shifted on his stool and looked away.

"Is that a rude question?" I asked.

"Ish? It's not like asking a woman her age or anything. But vampires… our society is full of schemers. Every statement, every question can be political. It's rare to ask these sorts of things outright." Victor turned his head and held my gaze. "It was 1888. That's the year I was created. The year I died, and became a vampire."

"So the clothes…?" I gestured toward him and waved my hand at his coat. "Have you always dressed that way?"

"I tried keeping up with the fashion at first. And I did for decades. But after a while, it got harder, and people thought I was eccentric anyway, so I leaned into it. I figured why not enjoy what I'm wearing? I always liked the fashion my parents wore when I was a young child, so I figured why not?" He tugged at the hem of his vest. "Waistcoats are swell."

I smiled at him. "I like it. It's very you."

He reached for his wine. "What else did you want to know?"

"I'm trying to keep my questions straight. Let's start with what you know about him. We've got an approximate age. And that he would have been hard to kill. What else do you know? Did he have any enemies? What emotion did he eat?"

"I don't know."

"Is there someone who might?" I sipped my wine. It was refreshing and tart.

"Maybe on the first one, doubtful on the second. Vampires don't usually reveal what emotion they eat to each other. It's one of our few weaknesses."

I ran my finger over the vampire entry again. "It says vampires can't starve to death but not eating can make them erratic."

"Have you ever been hangry?" he asked.

"You have no idea." Casting spells on an empty stomach was always a bad idea. The practice took a massive amount of energy, and a few times, I had overcast and ended up in the emergency room with low blood sugar.

"Well, imagine that but times it by a hundred. The longer we go without eating, the more we think about eating. It can become all-consuming. We lose focus. Anything that requires finesse? Don't even bother. We become so irritable that no one would want to be around us. And if it goes on long enough, we stop healing. Everything aches, and our heads pound."

"Almost sounds like a bad case of the flu."

He shook his head. "It's worse than that. We lose everything that makes us who we are, and all that is left is hunger. It's like our own personal hell that we can't escape."

"Do you know that from personal experience?"

"Not my own, but I've witnessed it." Victor bit into his garlic bread. "Vampires are vicious at times. Against each other more than anything else. We are long-lived. You're either lucky, like me, and find things in the world to be inspired by, or you try to find inspiration with each other. And that inspiration is usually Machiavellian. It's a game to see how we can prod each other into doing things. Because of that, most vampires keep their food supply a secret because they don't want to risk it being tampered with."

"So it would be rude for me to ask you what you eat?" I asked.

Victor chuckled. "Even ruder than asking my age."

"Have you—never mind." I stared down at my plate.

"Have I what?"

"Have you ever eaten my emotions?" I peered up at him.

Victor picked up his glass of wine and threw it back, his eyes bouncing around the room. He looked anywhere but at me.

"Never mind. It's... I don't need to know." *Do I? No. I don't. Yes. I do. I don't know. Do I?* I pushed the few remaining noodles around my plate with my fork. *It doesn't matter right now. Focus on what's important.* "So, someone else might know who his enemies were?"

He relaxed into his seat. "Yeah. There are a few people, but only one that I can think of that would be okay with me introducing you to him. He's sort of the local area gossip for the vampire court."

"Court?"

He grimaced. "Yeah."

I leaned into the table. "So, there's, like, a king?"

"There is." Victor eyed the wine bottle, sighed, and pushed his empty glass away. "Vampires never got out of the monarchy system. There's a king. He's intense. Don't worry. You won't have to meet him."

"I'll be meeting the gossip instead. Like a courtier?"

"More like a prince. He's the king's youngest kid." Victor took another bite of his pasta.

"Kid? So it's like a parental thing?"

Victor grimaced. "For some it is. Most of us just refer to those who made us into vampires as our creators, and we are their progeny. This king is more... affectionate? I guess that's as close to the right word as I'm going to get. He's more affectionate with his progeny, so they usually call him Dad, and he calls them his kids."

"Huh." I tore off a chunk of bread and nibbled at it.

"You should finish up. The prince is probably still at work, so if we head out, we might be able to catch him today."

"Work?" I asked.

Victor nodded. "He runs the local indie theater."

I grabbed my garlic bread and quickly ate the rest of my food while we continued to chat. Vampires weren't anything like what I expected. After this case was over, I really needed to spend a few days reading the rest of the field guide and try to find copies of the recommended books for additional reading. And maybe a few etiquette books, as well, if I was going to be meeting supernatural royalty more often. Plus, with Victor being from the 1800s, some more knowledge might keep me from putting my foot in my mouth around him.

# CHAPTER 8

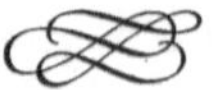

We opted to take one vehicle. It didn't make sense to take two cars. I drove because Victor's place was on my way home from the indie theater downtown. It had been built for plays in the 1920s and converted to a movie theater in the 1970s, with not much updating since then. The interior was gloomy, and the sign outside only worked some of the time. The theater didn't get any new movies in and instead replayed classics. On the single screen that night was the original *Psycho*. Nostalgia drew a consistent crowd of horror fanatics to the venue.

I trailed after Victor as he approached the ticket booth. The street was mostly empty in the lull between the dinner rush and the small night life of Point Pleasant. I hung back as he murmured to the man behind the glass. The man peered at me over Victor's shoulder. He had gaunt, angular features softened by dark-brown hair that hung in tousled waves around his face. He wore a *Nightmare on Elm Street* T-shirt and fingerless gloves, and his nails were painted black. He nodded and gestured for Victor to enter. Victor reached back and took my hand, and we strode inside. I walked quickly as we followed the guy up a set of stairs tucked behind a curtain to the left of the front door.

The steps ended outside a nondescript door. The guy opened it without knocking and stuck his head inside. "Switch places with me." He had an East Coast accent but not one I could place, like Boston or New York.

A few seconds later, a lanky teenager emerged. He wore a *Friday the 13th* shirt, and his shaggy chestnut hair stuck out at odd angles from under a beanie. He didn't make eye contact as he took the stairs down two at a time.

We followed the first guy into the room, and he flopped down into the seat next to the projector and pulled out a vape pen. "You've got ten minutes before I have to switch the reels."

Victor bowed at the waist, his arm gracefully extended at his side. "Prince Stokes. I thank you for taking time out of your busy schedule to speak with us."

"Us?" Prince Stokes's eyebrow rose. "And enough with the *prince* nonsense. We're not in court. Unless this is court business..."

Victor straightened and motioned me forward. "Alvin, this is Megan Miller."

I kept my expression bland as I stepped forward. Prince Alvin Stokes was not what I had expected. He looked a few years younger than me—with him being a vampire, it was impossible to tell, but he had a gothic, almost emo air that felt too recent for him to be old. Victor had described him as the king's youngest son.

*How old is young?* I glanced at Victor and did my best attempt at a curtsey.

The corner of Alvin's mouth quirked up in a smile. "Miss Miller, huh? What's she doing here? You finally looking for permission to make a kid?"

"No, I... no." Victor spluttered. "Megan's here on official business."

Alvin cocked his head. "No offense, but I don't recognize you as someone important. You new?"

"You could say that. It's subjective. I've lived here my whole life," I said.

He waved his hand at me in a circular motion, prompting me to continue.

"I'm investigating Manual's death. Victor said you might be able to assist me."

His eyes darted over to Victor, his expression darkening. "Based on that introduction, I'm assuming she isn't one of ours."

"Correct." I straightened further, my spine ramrod straight. "I'm a witch."

Alvin scoffed, tilted his head back, and inhaled deeply from his pen. He rubbed his temples as he slowly exhaled a large puff of vapor. "Did you miss the part about not airing our business to outsiders, Victor?"

Victor pulled at his cuffs. "We're signatories to the Accords. She's here on Warden business."

"Don't remind me. I can't stand that we gave authority to investigate supernatural crimes to a bunch of snobs." Alvin pulled his bottom lip between his teeth and gave me a calculating look. "And you need my help?"

"I do." I forced a smile onto my face. "I'm just trying to do my job. Find the killer. And then I'll be out of your hair."

He leaned forward, resting his elbows on his knees. "How many years have you been a Warden?"

"I'm not one."

His eyes snapped to Victor.

I held up my hands. "I'm a liaison for them. I… I'm investigating the murder on their behalf."

"All right." He relaxed into his seat, steepled his fingers in front of his face, and scowled at me. "So, how long have you been their lapdog?"

"Two months."

He laughed, his face lighting up, taking him from mildly threatening to delighted. He wiped at the corners of his eyes. "Oh man. Two months? Shoot. You really do need my help, then. I thought this was some sort of prank."

"Please," I said. "I just need somewhere to start. A name. A place. And I'll take it from there." *I hope.*

"All right." He shook his head, chuckling to himself, and slid farther into his seat, his legs widening. "I'm not sure how much help I can be. I only know of one person who had a beef with Manual, and I'm going to need to check with my 'dad' before I can share his name with you. Since you're not a warden and all. I'll make a call and get back to you."

"Is there anything you can tell me without permission?"

"Not that it's helpful, but sure. Manual's kid hated him." Alvin pressed his fingers into his temples.

"Are you okay?" I asked.

He raised an eyebrow. "Putting up with this nonsense would give anyone a headache."

I kept a polite smile on my face and ignored the jab. "Are there any other vampires I can talk to who might know more?"

Alvin's expression shuttered. "He's the only one you need to know about until Father decides otherwise."

"Got it." I took a step back. "Thank you for your time. We should probably be heading out."

"You can go," Alvin said. "But, Victor, we need to have a few words."

I stiffened. "I'm his ride."

Alvin smiled. "Don't worry. I'll make sure he makes it home safe. We've just got a few things to chat about first."

Victor pressed his hand into my lower back. "It's all right. I'll text you tomorrow."

I jerked my head in an awkward nod and exited the small

projection room. The door clicked shut behind me, and I strode down the stairs. I held my arms still at my sides until I made it back out to the truck, where I collapsed into the front seat then drove away, my fingers clutching the steering wheel.

Leaving Victor at the theater didn't feel right, but something about Alvin's direction for Victor to stay behind made told me it wasn't a request. The encounter had been my first taste of vampire politics, and I didn't like it at all.

I drove back to the farm in a daze and parked in the carport. I was barely out of my truck when Gertie ambled over from the barn. She was too smart to keep locked up for long. She could nose her way out of any latch and was offended by actual locks. I scratched her nose and leaned against her in the darkness.

Through our bond, Gertie sent calming emotions to me.

My fingers sank into her fur. "It was a weird day."

Gertie shuffled closer and rested her head against my shoulder.

"I got the case."

My heart swelled with the pride Gertie felt at my words.

"I interviewed two people. They were horrid. And learned about vampires. Did you know they eat emotions?" I stroked the side of her head and snorted. "But it's rude to ask what emotion. Which makes sense after meeting more of them. I'm not sure if I'm cut out for this one."

I sighed and pushed away from her. She followed me back to the house and took up her usual spot outside my kitchen window. I darted inside and rushed through the house to open it for her. She shoved her head through the window and snagged an apple from her snack bowl. I puttered around the kitchen, making myself a banana split. After dropping into my recliner closest to the window, I dug in.

Gertie grabbed a cow cake next and munched on it as I sat in contemplation.

"Victor didn't want to answer the question—if he had ever eaten my emotions before. I... what if he eats anxiety? Is that why he wants to be my friend—because I'm tasty?"

Gertie snorted and threw the remains of her cookie at me.

I swatted the debris away and glared at her. "It's a legit concern."

She stared at me.

*Except I'm usually not anxious when I'm with him.* I finished eating my ice cream. And even if I were tasty to him, I wasn't sure it mattered. He had taken a chance on introducing me to Alvin. My stomach clenched. I didn't want Victor to get in trouble. If Alvin wasn't going to give me the name, there were other ways for me to find it. I just really didn't want to ask Miranda for help. Hopefully, Victor's gambit would pay off.

I jumped as my phone vibrated in my pocket. As I fished it out, a second text message came through.

> **VICTOR:**
> I got the name.
>
> I've been given permission to make an introduction.

When and where?

> **VICTOR:**
> Tomorrow. Meet me at the high school at 4 PM.

I stowed my phone away and cleaned up.

"Good night, Gertie." I dropped a kiss on her forehead and closed the window.

As I approached my bedroom, I went through the day in my mind and started making a list of next steps. I would start by interviewing Manual's estranged kid. If that didn't go anywhere, I could try to track down the other members of the PTA to confirm Tiffany's alibi and see if Douglas was willing to talk to a different person. Illusion magic made starting over a possibility.

# CHAPTER 9

My stomach tightened as I pulled into the high school parking lot. I hadn't been here since a week before graduation. Back then, my powers had finally come in, and being around people had been difficult. I flipped my visor down to check my reflection. My usual impassive expression was in place. Unless someone knew what to look for, the tension lines around my eyes could be attributed to age or my vocation, not stress. I hopped out of the truck and made my way over to Victor's hearse, which was parked a few cars down.

Victor emerged from his vehicle. His black-and-silver tailcoat appeared to have been recently pressed, and there wasn't a hair out of place. His pompadour seemed taller than usual. He held out his arm and cocked an eyebrow until I looped my hand around his elbow.

"Who are we here to meet?" I asked. Images of the teachers or the school principal flitted through my mind.

"Henry Davis."

My body stiffened, and I moved robotically forward. Henry Davis was a name almost anyone in town would recognize. He started teaching a year after I left. I didn't know who I'd been expecting, but it wasn't the athletic director.

Victor led me to the athletic fields behind the cafeteria at the back of the school. Before we got there, I could already hear him. His loud whistle. The sound of feet pounding the pavement. His booming orders to go faster.

We rounded the corner, and Henry Davis came into view. Staring at him, I wasn't sure how no one had noticed. He'd been teaching at the school for twenty years, and he didn't look a day past thirty. He loomed over the field, his tracksuit stretching across his broad shoulders. His brown hair was cropped close to his head in a military style.

"You expect me to believe you want to make the team? Look at you! You're already slowing down. I expect you to give it your all out there. One more lap. Just because the school year's almost done doesn't mean you can slack off now." Henry rocked back on his heels, with his hands on his hips.

We continued to make our way toward him and stopped at the edge of the field in his line of sight. Victor raised his hand in greeting. Henry narrowed his eyes and marched over to us.

I craned my head back to keep his face in view as he got closer. He stopped a few feet away. Henry Davis would give Harrison a run for his money when it came to height. He was at least six and a half feet tall. Except unlike Harrison, Henry was broad.

He loomed over me, and scowled. "This is a closed practice."

Victor squeezed my arm. "I apologize for interrupting, but we are here on official business."

Henry crossed his arms and tilted his head back, considering me down his nose. "What sort of official business?"

"Miss Miller is assisting the Wardens with an investigation."

Henry snorted.

"And the king has requested your cooperation," Victor continued.

Henry ran his fingers through his hair. "What sort of investigation?"

"A murder," I said. "Of Mr. Manual Delgado Perez."

"Manual's dead?" Henry asked.

I nodded. "He was found dead at his bookstore three days ago."

Henry smiled widely, his eyes taking on an almost manic gleam. "Good."

I fought the urge to gape at him. I went through the questions I had planned to ask and landed on the bluntest one. "Do you know anything about Manual's death?"

"No," he said. "Other than I wish I could have been there in person."

I opened and closed my mouth. My other questions slipped out of my mind until the only one left was *Who says that?*

Henry shook his head. "If you knew him like I did, I can assure you, you would have felt the same way. He was a monster. The world is a better place without him. And the only thing I feel is glad that I don't have to share this town with him anymore."

"Did... did you see him often?"

"I avoided him like the plague." Henry glanced at the kids running drills behind him. "Manual moved here claiming he wanted to reconcile our differences and reconnect. Every time he stopped by, I told him the same thing. Not interested. He hadn't tried to ambush me with coffee in a few days, so I assumed he had finally given up."

"Was your relationship with him always that tense?"

"My feelings toward him aren't a secret." He stepped closer, pulling himself to his full height until I almost tripped trying to keep his face in view. "But that doesn't mean I killed him."

"Can you tell me where you were three nights ago?"

"Home."

"Was anyone with you?" I asked.

"No."

"Do—"

"Look, Miss Miller, I don't deny that I had the means and the motive." He ticked off the points with his fingers. "But I never had the opportunity. You said he was found at the bookstore. I've never set foot in there."

"Can you—"

"Prove it?" Henry scoffed again. "You're the witch. You figure it out."

I tried to keep my face professionally blank and hold in the glower, but it was hard.

He cocked an eyebrow at me. "Any other questions?"

"Can you think of anyone else who may have had issues with him?"

"Anyone who really knew him." He glanced back at the kids one more time. "If that's all, I've got a soccer team to coach."

I opened my mouth to ask one more question, but he turned on his heel and marched away, blowing his whistle.

"All right, kids. Take a breath, then break into teams of two. And Johanson, don't even ask about teaming up with Bradley again."

I shoved my hands into my pockets and watched him march away. I turned to Victor. "He seemed friendly. Is it normal for vampires to have such tense relationships with their creators?"

Victor placed his hand on the small of my back and led my back to the parking lot. "It's complicated. If you think about it, for us to be made, we have to die first. And it's our creators who do that. They destroy us in order to remake us. That's not a good experience for most."

"So it's normal?"

Victor grimaced. "I wouldn't say normal. But it happens sometimes."

"Do you hate your creator?" I asked as we stopped next to my truck.

"No. She was… kind. She thought she was helping me." He tucked a loose strand of hair behind my ear, and my breath caught in my throat. "Now what?"

I stared at him blankly. He had done that with my hair before, and every time it happened, my brain malfunctioned. He held my gaze, a question in his eyes. My mouth went dry.

*He just asked me a question, didn't he? Shoot. Shoot. He's going to notice me getting flustered over the hair thing. It probably doesn't mean anything, and I'm going to make it weird.*

I smiled sheepishly. "What did you just ask?"

"What's the next step?"

I blinked. We were standing close together. *Did I step closer?* I cleared my throat. The conversation with Henry had not been helpful, and all I could think about was Victor touching my ear. *Get it together. Focus on the case.*

"Let me think," I said.

All my conversation with Henry did was leave him on my suspect list without adding any new leads. My shoulders tensed as I went through my list of things to do. I still had to verify Tiffany's alibi and maybe try to reinterview Douglas. I paused as my thoughts drifted back to my conversation with Henry. "I've never set foot in the bookstore," he'd said. I might be able to verify that.

"Do you know where Manual's cat ended up?" I asked.

"She's still at the bookstore." Victor jerked his thumb over his shoulder. "I've been tasked with taking care of the cat until his estate can be figured out. I was going to pick her up on my way home."

"Mind if I tag along? I have a few questions for her."

---

Harborlight Bookstore was only a five-minute drive from the high school. It was the middle of the afternoon, so almost every parking spot in a three-block radius was claimed. I parked two blocks away and wandered over to wait for Victor. I stood, studying the collection of flowers that clustered around framed photograph of Manual. The photo was out of focus. Manual was standing behind the bookstore counter, holding up a book and smiling at someone out of sight. He looked so normal and happy in a woolen vest.

I studied his face. *Why does Henry hate you so much?* My gaze flicked from the photo to the flowers to a sign posted to the side of the building: "Point Pleasant Book Club Cancelled on account of Manual's memorial."

Manual seemed well liked. But Henry's vitriol had been intense. *Maybe he's a polarizing figure.*

Victor stepped up next to me. "You ready to head inside?"

I nodded, and he stepped around me to unlock the front door.

"Mariposa is upstairs. I didn't want her disturbing the crime scene," Victor said.

We treaded lightly through the room, careful not to disturb the debris that littered the floor. The faint coppery scent of blood had dissipated as it dried. All I could smell were books.

I followed Victor up the circular staircase and slipped into the office behind him. It was still cramped, and the cat odor had intensified. I glanced around the room until my gaze settled on Mariposa. She was in the same spot she'd been last time, tucked away in a corner under the desk.

I sat down in the rolling chair at the desk and lowered my hand until it hung in the space between us. Her eyes were already curious, and the first petals of my soothing magic had barely touched her when she scooted out from underneath the desk and sniffed at my hand.

"Hey, sweetie," I murmured.

She ducked her head under my fingers. Her fur was somehow softer than before. I petted her between her ears, tracing the outline of the butterfly pattern on her forehead. Her body vibrated as she began to purr. I muttered the words to the spell that would allow me to communicate with her.

The feeling was always a bit strange. Gertie was my familiar, so I sensed her in the back of my mind. She tended to be happy most of the time, and her presence was comforting. The connection to Mariposa was similar to what I had with Gertie but muted. It also came with flickering images in my mind as she considered my words. A half-empty food dish played on repeat as she rubbed herself against my legs.

I pulled up my mental picture of Henry and pushed a little bit more magic into my connection with Mariposa so she could see my thoughts for a few brief seconds. She stiffened under my fingers, then she continued with her pacing and purring.

"Mariposa, do you recognize that man?"

No images entered my mind.

I sat back. I'd expected Henry to have been lying, but the store cat didn't know him. *Although she didn't see the murder. It could have been his first visit.* My hand shook as I pushed more thoughts toward her, including the sound of his voice.

Again, no reaction. She had never heard his voice either.

I scratched her one last time between her ears and stood up so Victor could collect her. I didn't see where he'd gotten the cat carrier from, but he set it down on the table and picked Mariposa up to put her inside. My eyes tracked his movements then faltered as they landed on the table. *Something is different.*

I'd always been strangely good at those games of "one

thing is not like the other." I spent hours poring over *Highlights* magazine as a kid, staring at two images, trying to find all the differences. As I got older, I used the same skill with my memory of what something used to look like. It was helpful, especially when my powers had come in and so many kids had liked to prank me.

I closed my eyes and pictured what the room had looked like the last time I was here. *The leather-bound books.* I had moved them from the seat to the table. They still sat on the tabletop, but one of them was missing.

I placed my hand on Victor's arm before he could close Mariposa in her carrier. "I have another question."

Quickly muttering the words to the spell again, I reached into the carrier and stroked Mariposa's shoulder. "Has anyone been in here since I last saw you?"

Two images flickered through my mind. The first was of Victor as he filled up her food dish, and the second was of Douglas as he snuck in through the window and took something off the desk.

I smiled.

"What is it?" Victor asked.

"I just got a solid lead." I grinned up at Victor. "Douglas Howard was here, and he stole something. I've gotta go."

I patted Mariposa on her head and then darted to the door. This was the biggest clue I'd uncovered so far. I was mentally preparing myself, trying to figure out what illusion I should use to question him, when my phone rang in my pocket. I answered it as I exited the building.

"Hey, Megan," Chris said. "Ethan Bauer confessed."

# CHAPTER 10

I drove to the sheriff's station on autopilot. I didn't give myself time to question my decision to barge into the sheriff's station. I tried not to think about how I would justify that to the city council at the end of the week. Edgar was going to have a field day over this. Shoving those thoughts aside, I parked in a spot in the small lot out front and made my way inside. Peggy glanced up at me as I walked through the lobby.

"I'm here to see Chris." I strode past her desk.

She opened her mouth, shrugged, then went back to typing her report.

The door to Chris's office stood open at the end of the hall. I knocked on the doorjamb and let myself in. "I want to be involved in Ethan's interview."

Chris's head jerked up. "What?"

I pushed the door closed behind me. "He's a supernatural of some kind."

"Huh." Chris leaned back, resting his hands on his stomach. "He wasn't on Miranda's list."

"Neither was the victim." I pressed my hands into the top

of his desk and leaned forward. "He's supernatural. Trust me."

"Okay. Do you know what type?"

"I don't." I dropped into the seat across from him. "He's special." I gestured to my face. "He shimmered. It's not a shimmer I've catalogued yet. But… he's not mundane."

"Okay." Chris stood and tossed me a protein bar. "I was about to take his statement. Let's go."

I scrunched my nose. Protein bars were his wife's go-to snack for refueling after casting too many spells. I'd never developed a taste for them myself. I slipped it into my backpack and stood to follow him down the hall. As we walked, I straightened my spine and lifted my head until I was staring straight ahead with my shoulders pulled back. I instinctively added the slight stomp that kept most people at arm's length. I didn't know what I was walking into, and uncertainty always led me to put up walls and give the impression I was confident even as my mind whirled through all the ways things could go wrong.

Chris led me to the interview room. It was only a few doors down from his office and reminded me of *Law & Order*. The walls were plain, and there was a single metal table in the middle of the room. On either side were uncomfortable-looking chairs. A bare bulb hung from the ceiling, and one wall was covered in a mirror that someone could be standing behind.

Ethan sat hunched in his rickety chair. His teal hair hung limp over his forehead, and his gaze was focused on his hands, which he clasped in front of him on the table. A tremor ran through his body as Chris dropped a file folder onto the table.

"Are you ready to give your statement?" Chris asked.

Ethan nodded, his eyes never leaving his hands.

"All right." Chris sat down. He motioned for me to take the seat next to him.

Ethan's eyes flicked to me as he sat down. "Who's she?"

"Miss Miller is here to observe," Chris said.

Ethan chewed on his lip, pulling his piercing into his mouth. His eyes darted between us before landing back on his hands.

Chris flipped the folder open and picked up a pen. "Tell me what happened."

"I… I was standing in the horror section. I'm planning a road trip… was planning a road trip, I guess. I wanted books to read at the hotels. It was so hot." Ethan grabbed at the hair at the nape of his neck. "I could feel the heat on my back. And then I punched him."

I cocked my head. The broken shelves were next to the counter, not the horror section. *When did he move?*

"You punched him?" Chris asked.

Ethan squeezed his eyes closed. "I jumped on him and kept punching. My stomach hurt. My head was pounding."

Chris put the pen down. "Had you taken anything?"

Ethan's eyes flew open, and he shook his head. "My sister doesn't approve of drugs. She would be so disappointed in me."

*Wouldn't she be disappointed by him killing someone? This makes no sense.*

"Why?" I asked.

Ethan's head jerked toward me. "Why?"

"Why did you do it?"

"I… I punched him. I jumped on him. I had to do it. I… I don't know. He was in the way."

"The way of what?" Chris asked.

Ethan deflated and held the sides of his head. "I was in the horror section. It got hot. Everything hurt. I couldn't think. I was punching him. I did it. Isn't that enough?"

I stared at him as he rocked back and forth in his seat. Ethan looked fragile in this light. He wore a ratty T-shirt. His limbs were long and slender, and he had the hands of a pianist.

My gaze focused on his hands. No bruises. "Were you wearing gloves?"

"No."

"You don't have any bruises."

He pushed his hands under the table. "I know what I did. I punched him, and I didn't stop."

*Maybe he heals fast. Or is stronger than he looks...* "How much do you lift, Ethan?"

"What?" He stared at me, his eyes glistening with tears. "I did it."

"How much do you lift?" I asked again.

It didn't make any sense. He was stick thin. He shouldn't have been strong enough to kill a vampire by punching them. Not without being stronger than he looked. And not without leaving bruises on his knuckles.

"I don't like gym class," Ethan murmured.

I leaned back in my chair and caught Chris's eye. He nodded. The only two people who seemed physically strong enough to kill Manual were Bruno and Henry. Maybe Tiffany if she had a bat. But Ethan? With his fists? No chance.

"Do you—" My next question died on my tongue as the door slammed open and Rowan burst into the interview room, her rose-gold hair wild around her face.

Ethan's sister skidded to a halt. She pointed at Ethan. "Not another word until you have a lawyer present."

"I—" Ethan began.

Rowan rounded the table and pulled him into a hug. She smoothed his teal hair with her palm. "Not another word, you got me?"

Ethan nodded.

Chris stood and closed the folder. "We're still going to have to hold him for the night."

Rowan pursed her lips. "I understand. It's just… he wouldn't do something like this. It isn't him. He *didn't* do it."

I backed out of the room and half listened as Chris walked her through what was going to happen next. Ethan would be held overnight because he had confessed to a murder. Rowan nodded along and slunk out after making her brother promise to stay quiet and let her get him the best attorney she could find.

Chris led Ethan shuffling out of the room. Rowan watched him leave, her eyes red rimmed and her hands balled into fists at her sides. After he disappeared around the corner, she turned and strode out, her shoulders back and her head held high. I trailed after her. When we exited the building, I cleared my throat to catch her attention.

Rowan spun toward me. "What do you want?"

"You seem really sure he didn't do it."

"I know he didn't."

"How?"

She held her arms out at her sides and shook her head. "I know him. I know him as well as I know myself. He's a gentle soul. Honestly? Him confessing to things he didn't do is so on brand. He used to take the fall for all my screwups growing up. He's got to be protecting someone, because the Ethan I know? He would *never.*"

"Tell me about him."

Rowan pulled out her phone and showed me photos. She slid through picture after picture of them together, smiling and laughing. She paused on one of Ethan sitting astride an electric rocking unicorn and sporting a paper crown. He had a wide grin on his face.

As she scrolled, she described him to me. "He's fun. Creative. He likes to make people laugh. He's the older one, by eleven months. I've still got a year left before I graduate. But we're best friends, so he was going to take a gap year so we could start college together in the fall. He had this whole big trip planned. He's been saving up for it. He was going to drive around the country, visiting tattoo artists. He had this plan of getting a sleeve done, with each city he hit adding a new image to the design. He was only at the bookstore because he wanted something to read during his pit stops."

I nodded. "He sounds like a special kid."

I focused on her face as I said the word *special.* It didn't shift at all. I wasn't the best at telling when a person was hiding something, but my coven mate Dani had gone over a few of the things to look out for. She didn't stiffen or look away. In fact, she kept eye contact with me, like she was willing me to understand that her brother was harmless.

"He is special." Rowan held her phone up so I could see his face. "Everyone always thought I was the one that looked out for him since he's such a dreamer. But they didn't realize that no matter how terrible things got at our foster home, I always felt better after talking to him. I may have protected him physically, but he protected my mind. My soul. He's the kindest person I've ever met. He would never hurt anyone."

"Protect him physically?" I asked.

She gave me an unamused chuckle as she wiped her face then held up a fist. "Have you seen that kid? I would be surprised if he knew not to tuck his thumbs."

I studied her hand position. Her thumb was curled on the outside of her knuckles. It was a lesson I'd learned painfully when I was twenty-one. I had tried to fight back against some hecklers, and ended up breaking my thumb because I didn't know to keep it on the outside.

*But if he doesn't fight... could he be trying to keep someone safe?* My mind whirled as I went through the possibilities and stopped when I remembered my interview of Mariposa. *Douglas seems like a bad dude. Maybe he blackmailed him.*

"You're an investigator, right? Please, can you help me clear his name?" Rowan asked.

I squeezed her shoulder. "I promise I'll do my best to find the real killer. No matter who it is."

She smiled at me. For a second, she looked younger, like a weight had been lifted from her shoulders. She hugged me briefly before shoving her hands into her pockets and marching away down the street. I got into my truck and drummed my fingers on the steering wheel. Ethan's confession didn't feel right. Rowan thought he was protecting someone, and my money was on Douglas.

# CHAPTER 11

The roads were almost empty as I made my way up the coast to Oak Harbor. My hands ached from clenching the steering wheel. Every few minutes, a kernel of doubt wormed its way into my thoughts. Ethan had confessed. He was a supernatural. I could report my findings and be done with this. But every time the thought of turning around crossed my mind, I shut it down. An arrest hadn't been made yet, and I had a duty to continue pursuing leads.

I arrived in Oak Harbor a few minutes before five. I quickly parked and pulled down my visor to look at my reflection. According to the Shadow and Glasses website, the antique store would close shortly. I only had a few minutes to cast a spell and get inside before they locked up for the night. I murmured the words to an illusion spell and watched as my features shifted in the mirror. My hair became platinum blonde, and my eyes changed from green to a brilliant blue. I tackled my clothes next. Flannel and jeans became a silken blouse and high-waisted black slacks.

I stared at my reflection. I'd given myself an air of sophistication. The woman who stared back at me looked rich.

I flipped the visor closed and slid out of the truck.

Fighting the urge to stride, I swayed my hips. I hated to admit it, but I was channeling Miranda as I walked to the shop. She had a timeless quality and almost glided when she walked. I did my best to imitate her smooth motions.

*What should I say my name is? It should have an old-money feel. Alexandra, maybe?* My mind was still on possible names I when I entered the building. Glass flew across the room, shattering against the wall inches from my face.

My eyes went wide, and I dodged as a book flew past me. Gasping, I ducked and weaved as I tried to make sense of the chaos in front of me. A whirlwind of books, glass shards, and miscellaneous items swirled around the room. A wail unlike anything I had heard before pierced the air. And in the eye of the storm, clutching a metal tray, was Bruno. He swung the tray, battering the flying objects away, as Douglas whimpered at his feet, half under the table, gripping a wooden chair leg.

I flung myself down to the floor and army crawled across the room, my eyes darting around, trying to take in all the details. The wail sounded like a cross between a woman's scream and an explosion. I inched my way forward, one arm at a time, until I was within spitting distance of Bruno.

I grabbed onto a nearby couch and rose onto my knees. "What happened?" I yelled over the howling wind.

Bruno spun toward me and lifted the metal plate over his head. "Who are you?"

"Someone who can help!"

A flying stapler hit him in his gut, and he bent over, eyes watering.

"What happened?" I yelled again. "What set this all off?"

He swung the metal plate at a flying book, sending it skittering across the room, then squatted next to me. His hand slid into his jacket. Over the wind, I could just make out the whimpers of the dog inside his coat.

I held his gaze. "I can stop this. Just tell me what happened."

"Nothing. Everything was normal. Dougie was making tea. I was prepping to rebind a book."

"What book?" I asked.

He rose up a few inches and pointed. I popped my head up, my gaze following his finger. Sitting in the middle of the table was a leather-bound book. I ducked down before a pair of scissors could hit me in the face.

I frowned at him. "Is that the book you stole from Manual?"

He stiffened.

I snorted. "It is, isn't it?"

"Dougie won it fair and square at that auction. But the host gave it to Manual anyway. Dougie was only taking back what was rightfully his."

Another wail split the air.

The broken debris reminded me of the bookstore. *Could Manual have been killed by a ghost?*

I didn't have time to think about it as the couch flipped up and swung away from us. I scrambled to my feet and threw myself at the table. I grabbed the book and held it over my head, screaming the words of the only containment spell I knew. It wouldn't hold for long—I didn't know the ghost's name. But I could force her back into her book long enough to lock it away.

I continued to scream the words of the spell as debris pelted me. Translucent red rose petals exploded out of my mouth with each word. The petals swarmed through the air until they located their target. The form wasn't visible to the naked eye, but the petals surrounded the ghost so closely they almost gave it form. I slammed the book down on the table as the petals wrapped themselves around the figure and dragged it to me. The figure grew smaller and smaller as the petals squeezed it back between the pages. The book flashed red, and then everything was still. The books fell from the air, clattering onto the floor around us.

I turned to Bruno. "Do you have a secure room?"

"What?" he asked.

"Someplace I can put this." I held up the book.

Douglas scrambled out from under the table. "There's a storage closet this way."

I sprinted after him. The book shuddered in my arms, the ghost inside fighting its binding. I skidded to a stop next to Douglas and threw the book into the closet. He slammed the door shut and locked it. I raised my hands and murmured the words of all the warding spells I knew until there was a thick layer of petals over the door. Luckily for me, only witches could see magic. All Douglas and Bruno would have seen was the chanting.

My stomach rumbled as I slumped back against the hall wall.

"What was that?" Douglas asked.

I rolled my head toward him. "I'll tell you. But first, you've got to answer a few questions."

He narrowed his eyes but nodded. I followed him out to the shop floor. Bruno startled and picked the plate back up. "Where'd the other lady go?"

I glanced down at myself. All the casting had disrupted the illusion spell. The silk blouse was gone and had been replaced by my real clothes.

"Put the plate down, honey." Douglas walked over and patted Bruno's arm. "Her shapeshifting is only the second weirdest thing that's happened today." Straightening the cuffs of his shirt, he turned back to me. "How about a question for a question? And it's only fair that you go first, since you have provided an invaluable service."

I held up my finger and swung my backpack around to my front. I had disguised it as a cute little capelet. Unlike most women's bags, mine was filled with magic supplies. From the large pocket, I pulled out candles. I walked around the room, murmuring the words to a truth spell.

Then I lit four candles and placed one in each of the four corners.

I returned to the center of the room and held out a piece of sodalite to Douglas. "Hold this while we talk."

He turned the dark stone over in his hands and quirked an eyebrow at me. Normally, sodalite was dark blue, but if he lied while he was holding it, the stone would turn the same yellow as the flames.

"Did you have anything to do with Manual's murder?" I asked.

Douglas spluttered. "Absolutely not." The stone stayed blue in his hand.

"Hand the stone over to your associate here." I gestured toward Bruno.

Bruno glowered at me beneath his pronounced brow and took the stone. "No." It stayed blue in his hand.

"My turn?" Douglas asked.

I nodded.

"I think it goes without saying that ghosts are real." He studied my face while he spoke. I kept my expression impassive. He nodded. "And you are some sort of… medium… witch?"

"I am a witch."

Douglas's eyes gleamed. "What else can you do?"

I shook my head. "Asking if I was a witch was a question. It's my turn again."

Douglas bowed his head, smirking. "Of course. Please continue."

"The book I just put in your storage room—did you steal it from Manual?" I asked, motioning for Bruno to give the rock back to Douglas.

Bruno handed it over, his scowl deepening.

"Can you really steal from a dead man?" Douglas asked.

"Yes." I stalked to him and took the stone back. It hadn't

changed colors. "And I'm going to accept that as your question."

"What?" Douglas spluttered.

I snapped my fingers in front of him and exhaled a cloud of petals over him and Bruno. I swayed in place as the last of the petals left my mouth. Using this much magic was taxing. My stomach rumbled again, and I grimaced, remembering the protein bar I'd stashed away in my backpack. I didn't think my usual Snickers was going to be sufficient to refuel this time, so I was going to need to eat both.

I refocused on their faces and carefully infused the next few words with my will. I muttered the words to the spell that would allow me to alter their memories. I implanted a memory of them having an altercation with a mysterious man who wanted the book they stole from Manual's bookstore. I ended the memory with the desire to keep the book hidden in the storeroom and a simple command to not go in there for a few days. Each new layer of the memory made the hunger pangs sharper. Changing something this big was difficult.

Staggering, I made my way to the exit. I stood in the doorway and snapped my fingers to end the hold my spell had over them. Before they could turn around and see me, I ducked out of the shop and stumbled to my truck. I collapsed into the seat, my hands shaking, as I grabbed the snacks from my bag. I started with the protein bar, to get it over with, then moved on to the candy.

My investigation had taken an unexpected turn. And I still couldn't figure out why Ethan had confessed. *Unless he was possessed...*

I inhaled the last of my chocolate and started the engine. My hands still shook. The snack wasn't enough but would hold me over until I reached a drive-through. I pulled away from the curb, my mind only half focused on my destination.

While Douglas was firmly off the suspect list, he'd been replaced by someone else: a ghost.

# CHAPTER 12

I clasped the hot chocolate in front of me as Heather wiped down the tables at the Bizzy Bean. It was after closing, and only the two of us were there. The cats who made the café their home had been locked in their playroom for the night. Before driving back to Point Pleasant, I'd texted my coven mates, asking for an emergency meeting. We'd dealt with ghosts as a coven before, but we'd known who the ghost was, and we had a lot of backup.

I sipped my drink as I waited for Dani and Kim. It didn't take long. I had only been sitting there about five minutes when Dani unlocked the front door to the cafe, and she and Kim walked in. Heather finished wiping down the last of the tables, and they all converged on the booth in the back corner at the same time. Kim took her usual seat on my right, while Dani claimed the one on my left. Heather slid in last, claiming the seat across from me.

"What's the emergency?" Heather set a plate of cookies in the middle of the table.

I tightened my grip on my mug. "I'm investigating another murder."

Dani nodded. "Chris mentioned that. Didn't someone already confess?"

"Yes. But I don't think Ethan did it."

"Are you sure?" Heather pushed the plate toward me. She was trying out a new recipe for key lime thumbprint cookies. "Harrison came through earlier. He mentioned bringing that kid in. From what he described, it sounds like Ethan's pretty sure of his own guilt."

I picked up a cookie and took a bite. The filling was the perfect balance of tart and sweet. "I'm sure."

Kim pulled a notepad from her purse and dropped it onto the table. "Okay. That's enough for me. Tell us what you know."

I glanced between my coven mates. Warmth spread through my chest as they all looked at me with trust in their eyes. I didn't have to justify my belief. I'd told them I didn't think he did it, and they'd believed me. My lips twitched in a smile. I loved them like family, but letting my guard down was still hard. I appreciated when they reminded me why it was safe to do so. I leaned forward and went over everything I knew.

"Henry Davis? The athletic director's a vampire?" Kim asked.

"Yeah. He was a real piece of work. Even if he didn't do it, I can't imagine ever being happy someone's dead."

"Huh." She shook her head and jotted a few notes down. "That's surprising."

Heather sipped her iced tea. "As surprising as a haunted book?"

Kim nodded. "He's my son's coach. I never picked up a bad vibe from him."

"Maybe he shows a different face at school. I don't know." I sighed. "And the whole haunted-book thing is throwing me for a loop. I don't know if the ghost is a witness or a suspect.

But the amount of damage it did at Shadow and Glass? I'm thinking suspect."

Kim nodded. "I can help contain it until we figure out how to banish it. Any idea what its name is?"

"No," I said. "I didn't have a chance to inspect the book properly. The ghost is a prior owner or something. But we can't banish the ghost until I've had a chance to talk to it. If I don't, Edgar would have a field day with it."

"Do you think a séance would help?" Heather asked.

I exchanged a look with Dani. We both knew a séance spell, but unless you were a witch who specialized in necromancy, it only worked until the next full moon after someone died. I had a feeling this book had been haunted for a while. Ghosts got more powerful with time, and this one was too strong to be newly formed.

I shook my head. "The ghost's been dead too long."

Witches were almost always naturally stronger in one field of magic over the others. Dani specialized in divination —seeing the unseen or looking into the past or future. Kim specialized in abjuration magic, which was all about protection. My specialty, enchantments, helped me influence people's thoughts and emotions. The other schools of magic were transmutation, the school of change; illusion, the school of misdirection; evocation, the school of the elements; and lastly, necromancy, the school of life and death. Necromancy was the least common for people to be naturally strong at. While I dabbled in it, my knowledge began and ended with a few containment spells and a simple séance. The only necromancer I knew had left town six months before to start a job down in Oregon.

Kim drummed her fingers on the counter. "Let's call Izzy."

I glanced at Kim. Sometimes it was like we shared the same brain. Isobel Carter—Izzy to her friends—was a necromancer who had helped us in the past. "You think she would be willing to drive back up here?"

"Why wouldn't she?" Heather frowned. "It's not like she left on bad terms. She got a job."

I tensed in my seat. Asking people for favors made me uncomfortable. For years, asking for help had been a sign of weakness. I felt strange that it was now an option.

But Izzy was only a few hours away. *What's the harm in asking? That's what Heather always says. The worst she can say is no.*

I nodded. "Let's ask her, then."

Dani made the call. She put Izzy on speakerphone and placed her phone in the center of the table. In the background were muffled hammering sounds.

"Sorry. Construction of the hotel ballroom is running a little late." Izzy huffed into the phone as the click of heels against pavement punctuated the construction sounds. "Give me a second to find a quieter place."

"You're still in a hotel?" Dani asked.

"Yeah." Izzy yawned. "My friend owns it. The rent is cheap, and who knows if this temp gig is going to last or not. What's up?"

I leaned toward the phone. "I could use your help."

The construction sounds cut off as a door closed. "What sort of help?"

"Ghost help."

Papers shuffled, surprisingly loud over the speaker. Izzy cleared her throat. "I'm covering the grand opening of a new bakery. I've got an interview scheduled with the owner tomorrow. I'll need a bit of time to write up the article, but then I can come up. Can it wait until tomorrow night? If not, I can try to shuffle things around."

"It can wait," I said.

We disconnected the call and relaxed into the booth.

"Okay. We've got the ghost problem covered. I'll pop up

tomorrow to check on your wards. What else can we do to help?" Kim asked.

Dani tore a napkin into pieces as she thought. She had always been a fidgeter. "I'm sure you've already thought of this, but what if Ethan was possessed by the ghost? It would explain why he's so sure he did it and why his sister's so sure he would never."

"Is there a way to check?" Heather handed Dani another napkin.

I sat up in my seat. "Maybe. There would be something unusual about the memory, right?"

Dani nodded. Her daughter, Grace, had been possessed briefly. She described her memories of that time as being distinctly different from the normal ones.

I grabbed Kim's notebook and began jotting down ideas. "I could use memory magic. I've only ever used it to rewrite memories. But when I'm communicating with animals, I can see their memories, so maybe I could modify a spell to try and see a person's."

"Would seeing it once be enough?" Heather asked.

I froze, my pen hovering over the page. If the memory wasn't as distinct as Grace's, they might need multiple viewings to notice it. *Would the memory come out the same each time?* Memories could shift the more you repeated them. They were imperfect like that for most people.

"Could you record it?" Dani finished tearing the napkin up and started drumming her fingers on the table.

Kim reached for the notepad and jotted down a few ideas of her own. Protection magic worked best when it stuck around, so Kim had become proficient in tying her magic to physical objects over the years. Dani and I could do that as well, but it didn't come as naturally to us.

Kim glanced up at me. "What crystal is best for recollection?"

"Yellow calcite," I said.

She jotted a few more words down and then slid the paper across to me. I made a few more tweaks and handed it to Dani. She added a few notes herself. We handed the notebook back and forth for a few more rounds before we settled on a spell that I thought would work.

I leaned back in my seat. "Now I just need to get access to Ethan again."

"I'm sure you can convince Chris, but didn't Ethan ask to speak to an attorney? Do you think they will let you?" Heather asked.

I shrugged. Rowan had wanted my help, but if she had gotten him an attorney like she planned, it might not be up to her. *I'm sure if we work together, I can talk to him.*

"I hope so," I said and typed a message to Chris.

> I think I found a way to discover if Ethan's memories are legit. You think you can get me another interview?

> **CHRIS:**
> I'll do my best. No promises.

I glanced down at the notes Kim had taken during the first half of our meeting. There were four items on the to-do list.

*Interview and banish the ghost*
*Interview Ethan*
*Confirm Tiffany's alibi*
*Reinterview Henry*

My gaze traveled up and down the list. The first two would have to wait until Izzy arrived or Chris got me access. Tiffany wasn't high on my list, but her skill with a bat—and her animosity toward Manual—had kept me from crossing off her name. If she really did have a solid alibi, it would shorten my list of suspects considerably.

"But first, let's track down Miss Allen. Tiffany said she was making posters with her at the time of the murder. You guys game for a bit of social media snooping?"

Dani grinned. "That's always been my favorite investigative tool. Let's do it."

We all pulled out our phones. We started by looking into Miss Piper Allen, who turned out to be an art teacher for the town's elementary and middle schools. Her photos were bright and colorful. Half of her feed was filled with videos of *five-minute crafts* that obviously took more than five minutes to complete. Halfway through the search, Heather was jotting down ideas for things to make to decorate the café. She was forever running out of cat toys because of all the fosters that came through.

Next, Kim poked around, trying to find out anything interesting on Henry. His online presence was the definition of boring, with no photos of himself and a lot of football stats and feel-good posts about how well the various sports teams were doing this year. I could see why Kim doubted his placement on my list. His written words were almost nauseatingly sweet.

Once we had snooped around on Piper and Henry's pages, Dani and I attempted, again, to find anything interesting on Douglas Howard. After almost an hour, the only items of note were that Douglas was married to Bruno, that Bruno had gone to school for art history, and that they owned a teacup Pomeranian named Snowball. While Bruno and Douglas didn't have a social media presence, Snowball's page was very active. There were thousands of photos of this dog lounging around. With each one, I became more confused. Douglas seemed like a knockoff mobster in person. It was hard to reconcile that with someone who doted on a five-pound dog.

After an hour, Heather loaded me up with treats for Gertie, and we packed up and headed home. As I drove, all I could think of was my bed and my hope that in the morning, Piper Allen would be in a talkative mood.

# CHAPTER 13

Lindsey had finals the next week, so she texted me first thing in the morning, apologizing and saying she needed the morning off to study. Without her, morning chores took longer than normal. Gertie appreciated me being there and followed me dutifully around the farm as I mucked out stalls, fed chickens, weeded, and swept. It was past ten in the morning when I finally finished up and restocked my backpack. Gertie snuffled at it as I shoved a few extra snacks into the front pocket.

"Sorry, old girl." I scratched behind her ears. "I know I've been out of the house a lot this week. I promise to make it up to you."

Her eyes widened, and she gave me her best adorable expression.

"How about I try a new cow biscuit recipe? I could try adding some apple."

She rubbed her head against my hand. She was a sucker for treats.

I chatted at her for a few more minutes as I packed my bag and cut up fruit for her to munch before I headed out for the day. Piper Allen worked half days teaching art at the elementary school and then moved over to the middle school for the afternoon. If I wanted to catch her, the best time was during recess, assuming the school schedule hadn't changed too much since my time there.

Parking space at the elementary school was limited. There were spaces for the teachers and only a handful of spots left for visitors. After sitting in the waiting line, I snagged the last one and made my way into the building as the kids streamed out into the yard to play. I headed to the art room and paused in the doorway.

Piper Allen sat behind her desk. Her mop of curly chestnut hair was barely contained by a bright-red headband. She wore a floral printed top that was splattered with paint. Half-moon glasses were perched on the bridge of her nose, and her tongue stuck out the corner of her mouth in concentration as she cut up colorful papers.

I knocked on the doorjamb and stepped inside. "Miss Allen?"

Piper didn't look up and continued snipping.

I inched closer, slowing crossing the room, calling out her name again after every other step.

Piper was humming and dancing in her seat as she worked. I ducked my head to get a better look at her face. White headphones peeked out from under her hair. I took a few more steps and reached her desk. I knocked on the top.

Piper jumped in her seat, half surging to her feet before her knees knocked against the underside of the desk. She toppled forward, her arms going wide. Her right arm knocked into a cup of coffee, spilling its contents all over her desk.

"Shoot, shoot, shoot." Piper yanked her earbuds out and frantically lunged for a roll of paper towels in a cubby behind her. "I didn't hear you come in."

I darted around her desk, grabbed a few towels, and helped

her wipe up the mess. Her neat stack of papers was soaked through. After drying them as best we could, she flopped down in her seat and pinched at the bridge of her nose.

"Sorry about that," I said. "I didn't mean to startle you."

"It's all right. I must have had the volume up too loud." She looked at me between her fingers. "I don't think I recognize you. Are you a parent or...?" She stretched out the word *or*.

I fished out the badge the city council had given me and flashed it. "Megan Miller. I'm assisting the city with an investigation."

"Oh?" She straightened in her seat.

I nodded. "I was hoping we could talk about Tiffany Malone."

Piper groaned. "Look, I removed most of the books she wanted from the classroom already. But I refuse to remove every children's book that contains imaginary friends. It's asinine."

"No, I—not that type of investigation. I'm looking into a murder."

Her eyes widened. "That sounds like a longer conversation than I currently have time for." She gestured wildly at the ruined paper on her desk. "Unless you want to help me cut out a new stack of mini graduation caps."

I glanced down at the mess and sighed. "Sure, why not?"

Piper stood and found me a seat and a pair of scissors. The chair was designed for small kids. I perched on it, my knees at my chest, and followed her directions on how to cut the shapes she was looking for.

"We're throwing a big end-of-year celebration, and the kids are going to be making little graduation-party invites for their parents."

"Adorable," I said.

She chatted away for a few more minutes before I could

redirect our conversation to Tiffany. "She tells me she was with you four nights ago. Is that true?"

Piper squirmed in her seat. "If you want to call that *with me,* then sure."

I raised my eyebrows.

She sighed and put her scissors down. "We were up until almost two a.m., making signs for a bake sale. Parties like the end-of-school-year bash aren't part of the budget. We have to fundraise for them. Tiffany always lends a hand. But there are times when I wish she wouldn't."

"Like four nights ago?"

"Yeah." Piper wiped the back of her wrist on her forehead, spreading glitter across her face. "Tiffany is a perfectionist. I had to remake my signs fourteen times before she thought they were good enough."

"And she was there the whole time?"

Piper laughed. "How else would she perfect the art of hovering? She stood behind me, commenting on my scissor skills the whole time. It would have been faster for her to make the signs herself."

"What time did you start?"

She scowled. "Right after school ended. I sat in a room with that woman for almost eleven hours. It was madness. Most of the other mothers dropped out after two hours, but Tiffany? God. That woman was impossible. She probably held me here that long because she's upset about the books." Her voice rose in a mock imitation of Tiffany. "'I'm just worried about the children. What type of lesson are we teaching them if we make them rely on falsehoods for comfort?'" She pointed her scissors at me. "*Where the Wild Things Are* is a classic for a reason."

I laughed, but her expression remained serious. The laughter died on my lips. "She wants to ban *Where the Wild Things Are*?"

Piper nodded. "She thinks it sets a bad example for children."

"That's insane."

Her eyebrows rose. "Right?"

"Okay. So, four nights ago, you were with Tiffany all evening?"

Piper huffed. "Unfortunately." She leaned forward, whispering conspiratorially. "Is this about the bookstore owner? I heard she had a beef with him."

"I can't discuss an ongoing investigation."

"You won't hear about me spreading anything." She mimed zipping her lips. "I wouldn't want to give that woman one more thing to complain about. I've got her daughter in my art class for two more years."

We chatted for a few more minutes. She was animated with her hands and spent more time regaling me with stories than cutting. Fortunately, cutting out mini graduation hats from the construction paper wasn't hard, so by the time recess ended, we had a big enough stack again.

I ducked out of the classroom before it filled with children and strode out to my truck. I was about to pull out of the parking lot and drive over to the high school to interview Henry when my phone chimed in my pocket.

> **IZZY:**
> The interview was a complete flop, so I came up early. I'll be on the next ferry. You want to grab lunch first so you can tell me about your ghost problem?

I blinked. She had dropped everything to come help me. I smiled down at my phone as I typed a message back.

Meet me at the Slice of Life Diner.

My treat.

I entered the Slice of Life Diner and stopped at the counter. Almost every table was filled with customers, which wasn't a surprise, given that the two best chefs in town ran it together. Abby and Willow were masters in the kitchen. While Abby tended to handle the savory side of the menu, Willow's ever-revolving sweet side almost always featured pie-inspired milkshakes. I glanced up at the menu. One side was labeled Eats and the other Treats. Everything looked good.

"What will you have?" Abby smiled. Her honey-brown hair was cut into a cute pixie style. She had on her usual chef's coat and wore a splash of red lipstick for color. She was usually the one stationed at the counter. She had this ability to know people's perfect order every time.

"Surprise me," I said.

She punched in an order. "Coming right up."

I stepped aside for the next person in line and claimed a table in the middle of the room. Then I settled into my chair, soaking in the warmth of the place. Willow had collected thousands of photographs of the town and its inhabitants over the decades. Every quarter, she switched them out for a new theme. The current theme was celebrations, so every wall was filled with photos of happy people smiling wide for the camera.

While I waited, I checked the diner's website. There was a running poll on what the next theme would be. It helped drum up excitement. Willow had commemorated various decades, the seasons, and even unusual wildlife sightings. I clicked on Add an Option and typed in what I voted for every quarter—flora. I hadn't won yet. Gertie was a huge fan of flowers, so I did it for her. While she couldn't come inside, on the rare night when it wasn't busy, Willow would open up one of the windows in the back so Gertie could hang out and look into the diner while I ate.

Izzy arrived just as our orders came up at the counter. She picked mine up and brought it over, claiming a chair across from me. She handed me a lemonade-meringue-pie milkshake while she claimed the mango one for herself. The milkshake was almost the same color as her hair. Today, it was a warm orange with white tips, chopped into a messy bob.

I cocked my head. "That was fast."

"I called ahead." She took a long sip of the milkshake before leaning forward and dropping her voice to a conspiratorial level. "Willow posted that they were running low on mangoes. I didn't want to miss the opportunity while I was in town. These things are so good."

"I really appreciate you coming up like this."

She smiled at me, her dark-brown eyes crinkly at the edges. "Always. It's good to see you again."

"You too." I lifted my milkshake and took a sip. "How are you liking it down in Canyon Cove? I always thought if you moved away, it would be to a big city and not a town almost as small as this one."

"It's been great. Not as quiet as I was expecting. I'm just glad to be back at work. Even if, at times, it feels like I'm cheating."

I chuckled. "Cheating? How?"

"I write obituaries."

I tried not to laugh. A necromancer writing obituaries was funny. She did have an unfair advantage in that she could talk to the dearly departed when writing about their lives. "At least I know your skills are being put to use."

"That they are. What sort of ghost problem are you dealing with?"

I glanced around the diner. There wasn't anyone sitting near us, but to be safe, I murmured the words to an illusion spell. Anyone who listened in would think we were talking about our summer plans.

"Have you heard about my new job?" I asked.

She nodded.

"Well, my latest investigation led me to a haunted book." I described the scene I'd walked into at Douglas's antique store. I tried not to leave out any details so she would know what she was walking into. She was the only necromancer I knew, but she had just discovered she was a witch about a year ago. I wanted to make sure she wasn't biting off more than she could chew.

She whistled. "And you're sure you need to talk to this thing first?"

"I need to know if it's a witness or the killer."

She leaned forward and grinned at me. "Luckily for you, I've been learning a ton from my mentor. Lori is a fount of information. I know just the spell to help. This should be a piece of cake."

# CHAPTER 14

Downtown Oak Harbor was bustling. The sidewalks were crowded with tourists and office workers out to lunch. I left my truck in a small parking garage a few blocks from Shadow and Glass and walked over with Izzy to meet the rest of my coven. Dani was sitting across the street from the antique store with Heather and Kim. She stood as we approached and pulled Izzy into a quick hug. There was a round of hugs as Izzy went down the line.

Then Dani turned and pointed to the storefront. "Is this the place?"

I nodded.

"I popped in this morning." Kim grabbed her purse from the bench. "The wards were holding. The ghost should still be contained."

"Excellent." Izzy clapped her hands together. "So, what's the plan to get access?"

I smiled weakly. "Ask politely?"

She laughed. "Does that normally work for you?"

"Yeah. Perks of being an enchantment witch."

While asking for big favors would always be difficult, requesting small ones, in person, was getting easier. I exhaled slowly and mentally prepared myself. The last time I'd gone in there as myself, Bruno and Douglas had sent me packing with their attorney's business card. I could try an illusion again, but I wasn't sure how much magic this confrontation was going to take and didn't want to risk depleting myself. A polite ask, augmented by a bit of my magic, would be a whole lot less taxing than an illusion spell, which might or might not require the polite ask coupled with magic.

I clenched my fists and strode across the street before I lost my nerve. The bell above the door jingled as I entered. Most of the mess from the prior day had been cleaned up. The display cases were the worse for wear, and there were fewer objects on display.

Bruno looked up from a book he was reading and scowled at me. It was almost a permanent expression on him, like he had a resting annoyed face. I smiled brightly and hurried across the room to bring him into the range of my influence.

Bruno stood, buttoning his jacket. "We have nothing to discuss regarding Mr. Perez's unfortunate demise."

I stopped only a few feet away and widened my friendly smile. "I wasn't here for that."

He crossed his arms and stared down at me.

I exhaled a small trickle of my magic. The petals glided through the space and settled over his skin. *Trusting. You want to do me a favor.* I sent another ripple toward him to layer it on. His shoulders relaxed, and he dropped his arms.

"I wanted to look around for a bit, but I understand it's lunchtime. Why don't you go take a break and help me with my selections when you get back?" My magic pulsed around him. *Trust me. You can leave.*

He pursed his lips and rocked back on his heels.

I pushed a little bit more of my magic toward him and added a sense of contentment. *Everything's going to be okay.*

He pulled his wallet from a drawer. "That sounds like a great idea. Dougie? You hungry?"

Douglas popped his head out from the back room. "I could eat."

I gritted my teeth and moved past Bruno by a few feet to get Douglas into my field as well. I repeated the process with him until his body relaxed and he followed Bruno out the front door. I sagged against the display table.

A few seconds after Bruno and Douglas left, the bell chimed as Heather, Izzy, Dani, and Kim wandered inside. Kim flipped the sign on the door to Closed then walked back to the storage room I'd tossed the book into. "The wards are still holding," she said.

I straightened and joined the group at the door. "What do you need to get started?" I asked Izzy.

She retrieved a journal from her bag. Each page was filled with neat handwriting, each letter perfectly formed. In the margins were scribbled notes in a messier shorthand.

Izzy flipped through and stopped at a page. "I texted ahead. Heather, did you have any luck getting hyssop and wormwood?"

Heather swung her oversized purse around and pulled out a plastic tote that looked like a tackle box. "Already had both of them in stock. The amber was harder to find, but I tracked down a piece this morning at Moon and Mortar."

"Candles?" Izzy asked.

I patted my backpack. "I've got those."

Between the five of us, we had the ingredients needed. Dani and I always had our witch's kits on us, and as the coven's nonwitch, Heather took her role seriously and was always prepared to help. The parts of her purse not taken up by the tacklebox were overflowing with snacks. Kim relied primarily on crystals, which she carried on a beaded bracelet.

We scattered around the room, following Izzy's directions. I placed candles every few feet around the perimeter, while Dani followed me, burning wormwood. Heather plopped down on the floor with a mini mortar and pestle, grinding up dried purple hyssop flowers. While we prepared for the séance, Kim laid down a few more protective wards over the windows and doors. If things didn't go well, they would at least keep the spirit inside while we figured things out.

I lit the last of the candles and returned to the group in the center of the room. Izzy read over the spell one last time.

I crouched down next to her. "You ready?"

She nodded and set the book down, open to the page she needed. "Let's get this started. Let's meet the ghost."

I stood and approached the storage room. Kim joined me, and we linked hands. I had woven the containment spell into the wood of the door. Dismissing it took a little bit of effort as we had to unravel the binds. I mentally yanked my rope of petals apart. They disintegrated, and the door flew open.

Izzy started chanting behind me as everything that wasn't nailed down began to spin. A chair hurtled toward my head. I ducked, and it smashed into the wall behind me.

I scrambled across the room and took up a position next to Izzy, with Kim hot on my heels. I linked hands with Dani and Kim, shielding Izzy and Heather in the center, then poured my magic into Kim as she constructed a protective barrier of air around us. Office supplies pelted against it and spun away. A pair of scissors bounced off the barrier and were impaled in the wall.

Izzy inched up next to me and held the piece of amber overhead as she flicked hyssop powder into the air. "I beseech thee to calm thyself and speak."

Everything stopped midmotion. A pen hovered in the air two feet from me. Then it fell to the floor. A speaker installed in the ceiling crackled, and a woman's voice, garbled by static, came through. "Who are you?"

"My name is Isobel Carter. We have some questions for you."

"No," the woman responded.

Izzy snorted and flicked more hyssop into the air. "Yes, you will answer our questions."

The room vibrated. "If you promise to help me first."

I raised my eyebrows at Izzy.

She shrugged. "Must be even older than we thought. Ghosts get more willful with age. The longer they stick around, the more focused they get on what holds them here."

"Let's see what she wants," I said.

Izzy nodded. "What's your name? I would like to know who I'm talking to."

The speakers crackled again. "Promise to help me."

I cleared my throat. "We need to know what we're promising first."

"My work cannot be destroyed," she said. "I almost lost it in the fire. The whole city burned. My work needs to be preserved."

"Okay." Izzy stepped forward. "We promise."

A crackling sound filled the room again. I closed my eyes. It almost sounded like fire.

"I'm Lillian Whitcomb," the woman said. "What do you want?"

Izzy gestured toward me. "Answer this woman's questions truthfully."

Before arriving, I'd planned out what I was going to ask. Whatever I learned, I would have to report back to the city council in a few hours, and I didn't want to give them any reason to doubt my skills. "Do you remember where you were before this?"

Silence filled the room for a second. "A monster had me," Lillian whispered.

"A monster?"

"Hmmm. A hungry monster. He was always eating. But he liked books. He took care of me."

I nodded. She remembered being with Manual. "Do you know what happened to him?"

"An even hungrier monster killed him." She sobbed. "And then I was left. And then I was stolen."

My mind whirled. If she described Manual as a hungry monster, then the even hungrier monster could have been another vampire. *Henry.* "Was it the same type of monster as the one who had you?"

"Yes."

I cleared my throat. "How do you know?"

"They felt the same… just like all but one of you feel the same as each other." Lillian sighed. "It's lonely here. All I have time for is to think. To protect. To notice. They felt the same. They were the same."

"Do you know what this hungrier monster looked like?" I asked.

"I cannot see. The smoke. It hurts my eyes."

I sighed and lowered my head. I had a witness statement, but it wasn't strong enough to make a case.

"The boy may have seen. The boy would know," she said.

My head jerked up. "What boy?"

"The hopeful one. The one that took the pain away." She sounded wistful. "The boy would have helped me, but he could not hear me. And then I was alone. And then I was stolen."

I stiffened, my shoulders tense, as my mind worked through what she had said. Rowan said Ethan always made her feel better. *Maybe he was there.*

I need to talk to Ethan again. ASAP.

**CHRIS:**
Let me try talking to his sister again. What should I tell her?

That I need his witness statement.

**CHRIS:**
You really do think he's innocent?

Yes.

I shoved my phone into my pocket. "I've got what I need. Let's wrap this up."

Izzy made a few more promises of aid to Lillian then retrieved her book from the storage closet. It was a hand-drawn atlas that mapped out the greater Seattle area. The cover was singed at the corners. Each map was meticulous, detailing the geography and what lands were occupied by native tribes. It was a perfect snapshot of the region. The earliest maps were from 1884, with the last entry dated June 5, 1889—one day before the Great Seattle Fire. Lillian had died protecting her life's work.

"So, what do you think we should do with it?" I asked.

"Still deciding." Izzy placed her hand on the cover. "A promise is a promise, though."

"We could donate it to the historical society," Dani said. "I've done research at the one in Point Pleasant. I think Donna would treasure this thing."

We all agreed to the plan as we cleaned up as best we could. We headed out before Douglas and Bruno returned from lunch. Dani, Izzy, Kim, and Heather left in Dani's car, to donate the atlas to the local historical society. With it safe in the hands of a historical organization, Izzy was confident Lillian would finally be able to rest. I got into my truck alone. By the time I reached Point Pleasant, I was hoping Ethan would be ready to talk.

# CHAPTER 15

I drove straight to the sheriff's station. I had to give my update to city hall that afternoon and was hoping to have a breakthrough first. I was on the verge of something. The ghost Lillian had all but confirmed a vampire had killed Manual, and I was willing to bet Ethan was a witness. I grabbed a parking spot out front and made my way inside.

Peggy was in her usual spot, her red cat-eye glasses balanced on her nose. She smiled as I entered and waved me through. "Chris said he was expecting you. Go on back."

I nodded to her and strode down the hallway, my legs eating up the floor beneath me. The door to Chris's office was cracked open an inch. I barely stopped long enough to knock before pushing it open. I faltered in the doorway as my gaze landed on a person sitting across from him. Her rose-gold hair was messy and shoved under a beanie. As I entered, she turned, her eyes puffy and red rimmed. Despite the despair written all over her face, there was a fierceness in her eyes. Her jaw was clenched, but she released it as she recognized me.

"Miss Miller?" she murmured.

I took the seat next to her and twisted toward her. I

rested my fingers on her arm. "I need to speak to Ethan. I think I can help him."

She swallowed. "For his statement?"

"A *witness* statement."

She shuddered. "So it's true? You really think he's innocent?"

"I do."

She chewed on her lip and nodded. "I haven't been able to find a good attorney yet. If I did have one, I'm sure they would be telling me I'm making a mistake. Let's go."

I pressed my fingers into her arm. Talking to him would require me to use magic, and I didn't want his sister stopping things because I looked too weird lighting candles and using crystals. "It would be best if I spoke with him alone."

She studied my face. Her gaze shifted to Chris and then back to me.

"He'll be safe with me," I promised, leaning forward. I held my breath, hoping her protective instincts would land on trusting me.

She hesitated another second before nodding.

Chris stood. "I'll get him moved to the interview room."

I followed him out. He dropped me off and went to retrieve Ethan from lockup. While I waited, I prepped the room for my interview. I pulled out bundles of rosemary, sage, and mugwort and ripped the plants apart with my fingers. We were in a sheriff's station so I couldn't burn them. Instead, I threw the torn-up plants into my travel mortar and pestle and ground them together.

The leaves had just started to weep, the pungent, woody scent filling the air, when the door opened. Chris led Ethan to a chair then backed out of the room. His teal hair had lost its shine and hung limply around his face. His eyes were drawn, and his mouth trembled as he stared down at his hands. He didn't look at me as I walked around the room, muttering the words to a spell that would magically purify the space. I didn't think any large magical spells had happened here, but memory magic could be temperamental, especially when a person was trying something new, so I didn't want to take any chances.

"Ethan?" I whispered as I stopped next to his chair.

His eyes flicked up to my face before dropping down to his hands.

"I wanted you to tell me about what happened again." I fished a piece of yellow calcite from my crystal collection. "But first, I'm going to need you to hold this." I placed the calcite in his hand.

He stared down at it blankly. "Why? I did it."

"I know that's what you believe."

I moved around the room, wafting my hand over the bowl of crushed herbs. As I walked, I muttered the words of the spell the coven and I had written to help record a memory. I stopped next to Ethan and dipped my fingers into the bowl. Only a small amount of liquid had escaped the plants. I pressed my fingers into it and then wiped them across the stone.

I held my hand in front of his face. "May I?"

"What's this for?"

"It helps with memory."

He licked his lips. They were dry and cracked. "Okay."

I wiped the mixture across his forehead, placed the bowl down in front of him, and took the seat across the table. Then I reached out, lifted his hands, and placed them over my open palms. I muttered the final words of the spell. The translucent petals flowed out of my mouth, settled over the stone, and surged up to his forehead, creating a line of magic. At times like this, I was glad only witches could see magic. To Ethan, this all would look odd but not as odd as it could have.

"Tell me what happened." I squeezed his hands.

"I was at the bookstore. I wanted to get something to read

for my road trip. It was hot all of a sudden, and... I punched him. I jumped on him and I just kept punching. I was so hungry. I don't know. He was keeping me from something. And I kept punching." His hands shook.

"Is that all?" I asked.

"Then I was outside."

I slid my hand out from under his and picked up the stone from his grasp. I held it up in front of my face and peered into the crystal. It was mostly opaque, the shape of my fingers indistinct on the other side. I muttered the words to the next half of the spell. The color of the stone shifted, and an image appeared. There were bookshelves. In the image, Ethan's hands reached forward and pulled a copy of *Pet Cemetery* off the shelf. He flipped through it. The words were too small to see in the image. And then the room was on fire.

I almost dropped the stone. The shift was hard to follow. One second, it was books. The next, there were flames. I held the stone closer to my face, my eyes straining to make out the details. It wasn't the same room. The walls were earthen, like a basement.

*What the...?*

The image shifted again. Hands were punching down onto Manual's face. I squinted. The hands were larger and had heft to them. The skin of the knuckles was cracked open and bleeding. They were nothing like Ethan's hands, which were long and elegant. And without any clear transition, Ethan was outside, a block away from the bookstore, with his hands on his knees. There was no bruising on his knuckles.

My brow furrowed as I frowned. I repeated the vision, and it made even less sense. The transitions were jarring. I glanced up at him. "Have you ever been in a house fire?"

He blinked at me. "No... I... yes? I don't know."

"You said it was hot."

He scrunched up his eyes. "I had to save it."

"Save what?"

He shook his head, his hands going up to the sides of his head. "I don't know. What's wrong with me?"

"Hey." My heart lurched into my chest.

I hadn't seen anyone look that hopeless in a long time. It reminded me of when Kim had fallen and broken her leg twenty years ago. She didn't heal fast back then. While a normal person would have recovered in months, it took her years—a side effect of her magic being twisted by a curse she'd only recently overcome. She'd known she was going to suffer, and her heart broke, like Ethan's heart was breaking.

I reached out and grabbed his hand. "Look at me."

His gaze met mine, and a feeling of calm swept through me. He blinked, lurched to his feet, and scrambled around the room. "Where is she?"

"What?"

"That woman." He dropped his hands. "She needs to get to the hospital."

"What woman?"

"She was just here. She fell." He slumped into his seat. "Am I confused again? She was just here. Her leg..."

My jaw dropped. "Oh my gosh."

"She was right here."

I shook my head. "Have you ever remembered doing something you didn't do?"

"I—maybe?" He looked away. "My sister's always complaining that I protect her too much."

I pulled out my phone and opened a recent photo of me and Kim. I flipped it around to show him. "Is this the woman you saw?"

"No. She's too old." His eyes moved between the photo and my face. He leaned closer to the phone, squinting at picture. "But they look alike. Is that her mother?"

"That's her."

"How?" he murmured.

"Her name's Kim. She broke her leg twenty years ago. I was just thinking about it."

He pulled back, blinking away tears. "But she was just here. I saw her. Or... someone who looked like her, just younger. How... how is this possible?"

I swallowed. *If he freaks out, I can fix it.* I straightened in my seat, and tilted my head back. "I'm a witch."

"Wha—"

"And I'm fairly sure you're psychic and don't know it."

He clamped his mouth shut.

"I can prove it to you." I tried to smile at him to get him to relax.

His breathing was uneven, his eyes wide, but he still nodded.

I picked the yellow calcite back up and murmured the words to an illusion spell. Drawing on the memory in the stone, I recreated it in an image that hovered over the table in front of him. He pushed himself back from the table. He froze, his eyes focused on the image.

"That's my memory." He stared at me.

"Watch it closely," I said.

His gaze flicked back down as the memory started over. He inched forward, focusing on it as the images jerked from one location to the next. "Why does it look so strange?"

"Because..." I scooted around the table to sit next to him. "Parts of this are other people's memories."

He let out a strangled laugh, and a surprised smile crossed his face. "That woman wasn't here?"

I shook my head.

"And the room wasn't hot? I didn't punch anyone?"

"No." I took his hand. "But I'm hoping you might be able to tell me who did. Before this happened, did you see anyone else in the store?"

His head fell forward, his hair covering his face. "No."

"Are you sure?"

"I heard the doorbell, but I was reading a book. I've always loved *Pet Cemetery*. It's scary."

I held myself still in my chair. I knew the killer was a vampire. One with big hands.

"How am I supposed to know when it's my memories?" he muttered.

I squeezed his shoulder. "I don't know, but memory magic is a specialty of mine. I'll figure something out."

"Promise?"

I nodded. "It'll take some time. Until I do, maybe take a step back and ask yourself 'Is this something Rowan would believe I did?' She seems to know you well. If the answer is no, it's probably a good indication your mind's playing tricks on you."

He smiled at me. "She's the best."

"She really loves you. I'm going to need you to promise me something, though. Since I know you love her too."

"What's that?"

"The witch thing?" I smiled. "It's a secret."

"I won't tell anyone. Not even Rowan. It would make her worry more about me anyway."

"Okay." I squeezed his shoulder again and collected my supplies. "Let me see what I can do about this. And once it's all settled, let's talk. You're not alone."

He thanked me again. As I left, he sat there, hugging himself, his shoulders rolled inward and his head hanging low. On the one hand, I had given him peace. But on the other hand, he was still facing a difficult situation. He had confessed. This wasn't going to go away easily.

Chris stood in the hall, leaning against the wall. He straightened when he saw me. "How'd it go?"

I stepped in close and lowered my voice. "He's a psychic. The poor kid didn't realize, so the killer's memories and his got muddled in his head. He's innocent."

Chris pushed his hands through his hair. "Okay. I'll reach out to the prosecutor and see if I can get her to drop the charges."

"It's already gone that far?"

He grimaced. "My hands were tied. We had a confession. It lined up with what happened at the scene. And… we found the kid's fingerprints there. They had already been put in for processing when the case was given to you. The arraignment's scheduled for Monday."

I didn't have the answers yet—not ones guaranteed to survive town politics. My stomach roiled. All week I had been investigating with a deadline. Now it was here, and I had an even worse one looming only a couple of days away. "Then I'd better go put on my best song and dance for city council and hope they let me keep the case. I'm sure Edgar would prefer to go with the easy answer and let Ethan take the fall. But it's not over yet."

# CHAPTER 16

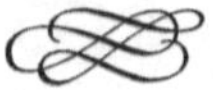

I was early. My follow-up meeting with the city council wasn't scheduled until four, but I wanted to get give them an update and get back out there to track down the real killer as soon as possible. I paced outside the double wooden doors, waiting to be let in. My footsteps echoed in the hallway. Between each step was the tick of the grandfather clock at the end of the hall. As I paced, I organized my thoughts. I'd had only had one big case like this before, and I wasn't sure if the council preferred a blow-by-blow update or the highlights only. Given how detail oriented some of them were, I suspected the answer was somewhere in between.

Miranda and Victor arrived a few minutes after me. Steven had reached out to them, letting them know the council would see us when they concluded their other business. The city council was in a closed session, discussing the Fourth of July celebrations next month. My hands were balled at my sides and my shoulders raised as I continued with my circuit. Victor took a seat on a bench across from the doors, and Miranda stood, regal in her flowing black dress, her jet-black hair braided in a crown around her head.

She was watching me with her eerie blue eyes, which made my palms sweat.

I turned away from her gaze and marched back up the hall, pausing in front of the clock and staring at the big hand as it counted down the seconds. *Start with the broad strokes. End with my findings from the spell. Support it with facts. I've got this.* I spun back around, and without looking at Miranda, I continued to walk back and forth.

After twenty minutes, the door opened and Helen stuck her head out. "We're ready for you."

I strode into the room, with Miranda and Victor trailing close behind. Chris hadn't arrived yet to give his opinion on the case. Helen padded back to her seat in her ballet flats and took her usual position next to Arthur. He stared at his pocket watch as she picked up her crocheting from the floor. Both of their mouths were pinched with displeasure.

I looked down the line. While Arthur and Helen seemed tired from a long day of deliberations, Edgar still looked fresh. His usual scowl was in place. He leaned forward, his elbows on the table and his hands tented in front of him. Steven had lost his jacket at some point during the day and stood with the top button of his black dress shirt undone and his tie loosened around his neck. Nicholas had his perpetual bored expression. He picked at his fingernails, with his feet up on the table and his hair mussed like he hadn't brushed it all day. Lastly, there was Mandy. Her suitcoat appeared recently pressed, her kitten heels tucked to the side under her. She tracked my entrance, her gray eyes gleaming as she shuffled papers in front of her.

"Do you have an update?" Steven flopped down into his seat.

I nodded and stopped in front of the banister that separated their half of the room from where their constituents would sit during open-door sessions. I stepped behind the podium and folded my hands on top of it to keep them from shaking.

"Is this entirely necessary?" Edgar asked.

I straightened to my full height and stared straight ahead, my gaze focused on a point behind Steven's head. "It is."

"Is this going to take long?" Arthur looked at his pocket watch. "I have a game of bridge tonight and was hoping to stop by the store on my way home."

"I don't want to keep you long." I gave my best professional smile and gave them a status update, quickly walking them through my investigation and saying I had cleared Tiffany and Douglas. I began to explain my interview with Ethan when Edgar cut me off.

"He confessed. The case is done. Why are we still talking about this?"

"I believe he's innocent. Ethan is psychic. He's obviously confused."

Edgar grabbed a file from the table in front of him and flipped through it. "Mr. Bauer isn't on the list provided to us by Miranda."

"Neither was the victim," I said.

Edgar scoffed. "Which is why I still believe it shouldn't have been on your desk in the first place."

"I admit our list is incomplete," Miranda cut in. "It's possible this boy is a psychic as Miss Miller claims. The list is a living document. Names can always be added."

I glanced at Miranda. "He is one."

She ducked her head in acknowledgment.

Mandy slid her hand forward, her fingers pressed into the wood of the table. "Just how many preternaturals have slipped through the cracks? Is this something we should be concerned about? I'm worried this list is worthless if it's this incomplete."

Miranda peered down her nose at Mandy. "You can't expect us to take into account every single minor talent."

"If they need special handling, then yes, I can and do expect it," Mandy responded.

"We're getting off track. Ethan is—" I began.

"Why shouldn't we expect you to track the minor talents?" Edgar asked.

Miranda glowered at him and muttered, "We don't typically consider them part of our jurisdiction."

A light went on in his eyes, and he turned his head toward his colleagues. "Well, then, if they wouldn't normally consider this part of their jurisdiction, why should we?"

"But—" I started.

"The victim is still a vampire," Victor said.

The room went quiet.

"That hasn't changed. It should still be on Miss Miller's desk," Victor continued. "Miss Miller, have you completed your investigation?"

"No," I said.

"Well, that settles it, then." Miranda turned to leave. "I look forward to the next update."

Edgar cleared his throat. "Remind me again what your role is, Miss Miller? I thought it was to triage cases and determine if the culprit should be dealt with by the Wardens or go through our legal system."

"That's correct. And I—"

"Someone has confessed. There has been an arrest." Edgar ticked off his fingers. "The culprit is not in the Wardens' jurisdiction. The arraignment is on Monday. Why are we still here? This should be moved to the sheriff's office immediately for continued handling."

"But—"

Edgar sighed. "I move to close this case on Miss Miller's desk. We don't need to continue wasting her time on it."

Nicholas straightened in his seat, his eyes bouncing between us. "We should listen to what she has to say."

Arthur snorted and shook his head. "Seconded."

Steven pinched the bridge of his nose. "The motion has been taken to the floor. Arthur, how do you vote?"

"I concur. If this case would historically be handled by the sheriff's office, then it should be there."

The votes went down the line. Helen gave me an apologetic smile as she agreed. The only councilor who voted to keep my investigation going was Nicholas. He pressed his index finger into the wood as he cast his vote. "For the record, please note that I formally object to this. We hired her to be the expert and are disregarding her opinion because of convenience."

"Your objection is noted." Steven stood and grabbed his jacket. "And for the record, I agree."

Arthur gathered his things. "Well, if that's all for this, I have a bridge game to get to."

My heart pounded as I turned and walked out of the room with my head held high before any of them could exit. Victor and Miranda trailed after me. We stopped when we reached the sidewalk.

Miranda patted my arm. "Better luck next time."

I stiffened and nodded. She walked away down the street without another word, leaving Victor and me alone.

"Are you okay?" he asked.

"Yeah. I don't know what I was expecting, but it wasn't that."

He wrapped his arm around my shoulders and squeezed. "You did your best."

*I should have had the answer before I walked into the room. I had a full week.* I nodded stiffly. "Maybe it'll come back to me. Ethan is retracting his confession."

"Maybe." He rubbed my arm and stepped back. "I'll see if there's something else I can find in the autopsy."

"I thought you already finished it."

"I did." He straightened his cuffs. "But it doesn't hurt to

take a second look. I have the weekend until the body is released."

"Thank you. I know he didn't do it. I know it was a vampire. I just don't know how to prove it."

"How do you know it was a vampire?" he asked.

"A witness statement from a ghost."

"All right." He held my gaze. "Then at least I know what to look for. I'll let you know if I find anything."

He turned on his heel and strode away, leaving me alone on the sidewalk. I stared after Victor's form retreating down the street, blinking back moisture. I hadn't been fast enough. If I'd figured out it was another vampire sooner, this would have gone differently. But I couldn't even tell the council for sure who the killer was. I wiped my face and jabbed a text message into my phone.

I lost the case.

**HEATHER:**
What happened?

The DA opted to prosecute. Ethan's being arraigned on Monday.

**KIM:**
What? But he's not a vampire.

I know.

**DANI:**
Then don't stop.

I lost the case.

**DANI:**
So? I never officially had the case when I investigated. Don't let city council be your Bob.

I stared at my phone. Bob Wright had been the prior

sheriff. He'd tried to stand in the way of Dani's investigations. She'd never let him stop her.

You're right.

I shoved my phone into my pocket and strode to my truck. I wasn't about to let Edgar, or anyone else on the city council, be my Bob. They weren't going to stand in the way of the truth. Ethan was innocent. When the case against Ethan fell apart, which it would, I would be there with the name of the real culprit. I just needed to get a confession out of Henry.

# CHAPTER 17

The parking lot at the high school was full. I found a spot on the street and parallel parked. It was another warm day. I was still shaken from my meeting at city hall, so I gave myself a moment to enjoy the feel of the sun on my skin and the scent of freshly cut grass. I closed my eyes and tried to visualize how the confrontation with Henry was going to go. Heather swore by visualization. She insisted that putting out positive thoughts made things better. *Maybe if I was a more positive person....* Every time I tried, my thoughts spiraled to the worst-case scenario. I would confront Henry, he would confess, and then he'd go on a rampage across campus. Or I would confront him, and he would laugh and poke holes in my theories. Suddenly, I would be surrounded by every high school bully, and they would join in. It wasn't logical. But that was where visualization always took me.

I shook off the mental image and strode toward the school. A whistle blew as I rounded the corner to the athletic field out back. Kids moved up and down the field, doing drills with soccer balls. Standing with his hands planted on his hips, periodically blowing the whistle, was Henry. With each blast, the kids turned and started back the way they had come.

My palms were sweaty as I made my way to him. He had on red athletic shorts, white socks, sneakers, and a white polo shirt. With his hands on his hips, his shoulders appeared even broader, the muscles in his arms straining against the material.

My mouth went dry. Despite my attempts at visualization, I hadn't fully planned out this confrontation. I had more time, but I couldn't think about anything other than coming here and looking him in the eye. Ethan was counting on me. Rowan was counting on me. I had to get this done.

I raised my hand to get his attention.

He blew his whistle again, and the kids turned around and moved away from him, dribbling the balls with their feet as they ran. He glowered at me as I approached.

"Miss Miller," he grunted.

"Mr. Davis." I stopped a few feet from him and stood with my feet wide apart and my hands loose at my sides in case I needed to cast any last-second defensive spells. "I had a few questions for you."

He snorted and looked away. "I answered all your questions when you were here last. I don't know anything."

"Your king wants you to cooperate with me."

He blew his whistle again. "I have."

"Tell me about your relationship with Manual."

"I'd prefer not to." He craned his neck and tracked the kids with his eyes as they ran back toward us. "I've got practice going on."

"That's not very cooperative of you."

His gaze flicked to me. "My relationship, or lack thereof, with Manual is irrelevant."

"I'll be the judge of that."

The group of kids came to a stop twenty feet behind me.

Their happy voices were punctuated by gasping breaths as they flopped down onto the grass.

An excited voice gasped from behind me. "Meg?"

Sweaty arms swept me up into a hug and swung me up and around. Conner, Kim's son, had grown a lot over the last year and had almost half a foot on me. "Where's Gertie? Has she come to watch me practice again?"

I tried to keep track of Henry as Conner spun me. "Put me down."

Conner was overly exuberant on the best of days and at the moment seemed particularly rambunctious. He set me down and stepped back. He was a golden retriever in the shape of a teenage boy. His golden-blond hair shone, and his blue eyes bounced from me to the field and back again.

"I've been telling the guys all about her. They didn't believe me when I told them a cow could play soccer. Where is she?" he asked.

I patted Conner's shoulder. "At home."

He sighed. "A guy can dream, right? You should bring her around so these knuckleheads know I'm not lying."

Henry smothered a chuckle. "A cow playing soccer?"

I crossed my arms. "She's talented."

Playing soccer was a bit of a stretch. Gertie knew how to kick a ball around and could run up and down the field with it. Her aim, for kicking it into goals, left much to be desired. But she'd still had a blast the few times Conner had brought his balls to the farm. And the fact that she could score a goal on occasion was impressive.

Conner looked between me and Henry. "So, what are you doing here?"

"She was just leaving," Henry said.

"No." I lifted my chin. "We're not done."

Conner lowered his head and whispered into my ear, "Why are you mad at Coach?"

My fingers dug into my arm. "I'm investigating a murder."

"And…?" Conner asked.

"And he's a person of interest."

Conner snorted. "Coach Davis?" He stepped back and shook his head. "No way. He can be tough, but he's, like, the nicest guy I know."

I cocked an eyebrow.

Conner held up three fingers. "Scout's honor. And you told me once I was a good judge of character."

"That's because you didn't like Bob."

He nodded solemnly. "And I stand by that. Even if he did get better."

"You expect me to believe Mr. Davis is… nice?" I asked, gesturing at him.

Henry crossed his arms and loomed over me, his lip pulled back on one side. "Jocks can be nice."

Conner nodded. "I mean, I'm nice, right? Plus. He's always looking out for us. He's great. The best. If you need a character witness, I'm your guy. I can't imagine him doing anything wrong, so you can go ahead and take him right off whatever list you've got going."

Henry clapped his hand onto Conner's shoulder. "Thanks for the vote of confidence. I've got this."

Conner glanced between us again. "All right, Coach." He ducked his head and ran back to the rest of the team.

I stepped closer and lowered my voice. "If you're such a stand-up guy, then help me understand."

He inched forward and whispered back, "I don't know what my relationship with Manual has to do with your investigation. It's history. Long gone."

"I know a vampire killed Manual."

His eyes widened. "And I happen to be one, so you think it was me? Not all vampires are monsters."

"I didn't say they were. I'm friends with Victor, remember? But one of them in town is. And if it's not you, then who is it? You haven't exactly been trying to clear your name. If the history between you really is meaningless, then what's the harm in sharing it?"

"You're right. There was a monster in town. Emphasis on *was*. He's dead now. Manual was not a good guy. Don't fall for his 'I'm just a bookstore owner' gimmick. He was controlling on the best of days and a narcissist who enjoyed hurting people on the worst. I wouldn't be surprised if he had a slew of kids out there who hated his guts." He glanced over my shoulder and yelled, "Take a cool down jog, and stretch out! Fifteen minutes, then hit the showers!"

"How many kids did he create?"

Henry shrugged. "I never bothered to ask. My creation wasn't exactly ideal."

"Tell me about it."

He sighed and visibly deflated. "He was a guard at Andersonville. Do you know what that place was?"

I narrowed my eyes and shook my head.

"A prisoner of war camp for Union soldiers. Manual was a Confederate soldier back then."

"And you...?"

"A prisoner."

I swallowed. Now that he mentioned it, I vaguely recalled hearing about Andersonville in a U.S. history class. If I remembered it correctly, the place was abhorrent and left thousands dead. "And he created you there?"

He nodded. "He enjoyed being a guard there. It was like an all-you-can-eat buffet for him. Now do you understand why I would want nothing to do with him?"

"That doesn't mean you didn't kill him." I held his gaze. "Let me see your hands."

He held them out. They were large. The knuckles were scarred, but there were no signs of recent trauma. *Victor said vampires heal quickly, so this might be meaningless.*

"Look, I... I can't necessarily prove I didn't do it. I know I didn't, which is why I know you can't prove I did. But maybe

I can give you a bit more perspective on who I am so you can realize it wasn't me. Before I do, though, I'll need you to promise me something."

I had been promising people things this whole investigation. *What's one more?* "Okay."

"Promise me you won't reveal what I'm about to tell you to anyone. Ever. It's private."

I nodded.

"Did you know that what vampires feed on is the strongest emotion present when they die?"

"I thought it might be something like that, but I wasn't sure.."

"Andersonville was awful. By the time I died, all I had left was hope."

"Hope?" I murmured.

"Hope." He nodded. "That's what I feed on. Was there anything hopeful about how he died? I doubt it."

"The vampire that killed Manual was starving."

He held his hands out and motioned around him. "I'm at a high school. I teach sports. I help kids get athletic scholarships. Every day I help them reach for their dreams. There's nowhere more hopeful than here."

I glanced behind me at the kids stretching out. Almost all of them had wide smiles and were joking with each other. Graduation was two weeks away. They were on the cusp of the rest of their lives. Hope shone out of all their faces.

"If it wasn't you, then who?" I asked.

Henry shrugged. "I've largely kept out of vampire politics. You would have to ask Alvin."

I nodded and stepped away. "Thank you for your cooperation."

Henry pressed his lips together and nodded.

I marched back to my truck, his whistle blowing behind me. I tentatively removed Henry from my suspect list. He was right—the scene of Manual's death hadn't felt hopeful.

Assuming he wasn't lying to me about what he ate, there was no reason for Henry to be there other than revenge, and that hadn't been what drove the perpetrator in the memory Ethan shared with me. Everything I saw in that piece of yellow calcite was desperate. Another vampire out there was responsible, and hopefully, Alvin would be able to point me in the right direction.

# CHAPTER 18

A matinee showing of *The Exorcist* was getting out as I arrived. I reapplied the spelled eyeshadow that let me see if a person was supernatural or not. It didn't last as long as I would have liked. It probably didn't help that I frequently forgot I had it on and rubbed my eyes. As I got out of my truck, my gaze swept over the crowd of people as they surged out the front doors, an extra-large group despite it being early afternoon. Most of them appeared to be regular humans, though the occasional person had a slight shimmer to their skin. None of them shone brightly, and if I hadn't been looking for the shine, I would have missed it. The shimmer reminded me of Ethan and Abby. I was beginning to recognize it as a low-level psychic ability. None of them had the same red sheen as Victor.

I strode across the walkway, winding my way through the crowd. In the first rush of people leaving was a group of rowdy college kids costumed as characters from the movie. There were at least seven guys dressed as Catholic priests, two women in white dresses with green goop painted down their fronts, and another in a turtleneck dress and a blond wig. The group stopped in the middle of the sidewalk, their voices loud and their excitement palpable despite a few slurred words. I weaved through them, trying to ignore the strong scent of beer and texting my coven about the change in direction my investigation had taken.

I tentatively cleared Henry.

**KIM:**
About time. It always felt weird having him on the list.

What are you going to do next?

Try and get another name from my vampire contact.

**HEATHER:**
I wonder what the next one's going to be. Hopefully not another pillar of the community. Henry was not what I pictured at all when you first said vampire.

Although I wonder if their long lives make it so they're more likely to be that. I guess if you've got nothing but time on your hands, it's almost inevitable.

Oooh. You never did explain why they can go out in the daylight.

I'll tell you more about them later. They are not what I expected either.

**DANI:**
Good luck!

Megan: Thanks. Hopefully—

"Still one of the best spider walks I've ever seen. I can't believe they cut it out of the original. It adds so much to the film." One of the patrons dressed in a polyester priest costume swung his arm wide, bumping into me as he walked backward. I fell to the side and slammed into the planter box. My phone flew from my grasp and landed screen down under the sprawling fern leaves.

"Oh gosh, I'm sorry! I didn't see you there." He grinned as he reached out to steady me. "Unfortunately, I haven't perfected the art of turning my head three hundred sixty degrees."

Another guy, dressed in a similar cheap costume, burst out laughing. "If you had, I would be the first to call a priest."

One of the girls in a white baby doll outfit, the green goo starting just under her chin, elbowed him. "You would not. You'd be the first one to pull out your phone to tape it."

"But in all seriousness," the guy who almost plowed me over said, "are you all right?"

I smiled and brushed them off. "No worries."

The group gave me a few more apologies before they wandered away to a bar down the street. I turned to the planter box and patted around for my phone. The planter had been newly filled. The dirt was loose and wet from recent watering. I winced as a piece of gray perlite lodged itself under my nail. Grumbling, I grabbed my phone and wiped the dirt from its face, only managing to push the mud around, my fingers too dirty to do much good. I approached the ticket booth.

A kid, maybe twenty years old, sat behind the glass, manning the booth. His shaggy chestnut hair was pulled into a tiny ponytail with half the hair escaping out the sides. There was a line across his forehead from where he must have taken off a hat. I smiled as I approached him. It was the same guy who had operated the projector during my last visit. He didn't have a shimmer to his skin either. He smiled at me as I stopped in front of the booth. I glanced down at his name tag.

"Hi, Mason. Is Alvin available?" I asked.

He glanced behind me, and I turned to look. Half the patrons were still clustered around the sidewalk, chatting about what movies were going to be playing next week. The next film wasn't starting for another hour, so there was no one in line for a ticket.

"No, sorry. He's been under the weather all week. Fighting off a flu or something. He's probably upstairs in his apartment."

"Oh, um..." I faltered as my mind scrambled for what to do next.

"Wait. Aren't you that lady who came to see him the other day?" He peered at me through the glass. "He never takes people up into the projection room. It must have been an important conversation."

I smiled weakly. "You could say that."

"Huh. Is this one also important?"

"Even more so."

He slipped a sign onto the counter that said he would be back in five minutes. "I'll check to see if he feels up to coming down. It shouldn't take long."

"That sounds great." I held up my dirt-covered hands. "Can I pop in to use your restroom?"

"Sure thing." He stepped out of the booth and beckoned me inside with a wave of his hand.

I pushed through the doors. Mason pointed to the bathroom before disappearing behind a curtain to the right of the booth. There was something nostalgic about the red curtains and dark wooden floors. The walls were covered with movie posters that spanned the decades, from the classic *Frankenstein* to the *Night of the Living Dead*. The newest one was *The Grudge*. I walked past them, my mouth watering as the scent of popcorn filled the air.

I made my way over to the bathroom. The wood floors gave way to black-and-white subway tiles. The room was dimly lit by Edison bulbs. I stopped in front of the sink. I was alone in the room. I slouched forward and rested against the counter. This week had been a constant sprint from one obligation to another. I studied myself in the glass. There were shadows under my green eyes, and my hair had come loose from its ponytail. I looked like a mess.

*I could take the weekend off. Nothing's going to happen until Monday.* But I couldn't shake the image of Ethan's eyes as he realized it wasn't him. The expression in them was half-hopeful and half-despairing over being arrested for a crime he didn't commit.

When my magic had first come in, everything around me twisted. People had distrusted me on sight. I knew what it was like to be detained over nothing and confess to things that I didn't do, hoping I was making the right decision. I never had the guilt Ethan carried, but the weight was similar.

I straightened. "I can't leave him there."

I dropped my backpack on the floor and turned on the faucet. The water was cold. I pecked out a few quick texts as I waited for it to heat up.

Sorry. Dropped my phone. Checking in with my contact now. I'll keep you updated.

Kim gave my message a thumbs-up.

I opened another thread to Victor.

I cleared Henry.

Looks like Alvin has the flu. In case he isn't up to talking, are you sure there aren't any other vampires I can chat with?

I tested the water. It was lukewarm. I set my phone down on the counter and pumped soap onto my hands. I froze. *That smell.* Inhaling deeply, I raised the soup toward my face. *Floral.* I glanced behind me to make sure I was alone in the bathroom. No one was there. I murmured the words to the spell that would transform my olfactory senses into a bear's. My nose looked ridiculous in the mirror as it became black and squished against my face, my nostrils widening. I sniffed again. It was definitely familiar. It was the scent of flowers I'd smelled at Harborlight Books.

My phone pinged. I glanced down at it.

**VICTOR:**
Vampires don't get the flu.

My heart skipped a beat. *Then why is he sick?* Passages from the field guide flashed through my mind. Victor had described what it was like to starve. At the time, I'd thought the symptoms sounded almost flu-like.

*When we first met, did Alvin have a headache? He kept pressing his fingers into his temples. And he was wearing gloves. Gloves in the middle of summer. I need to come back with a plan.*

My eyes widened, and I pushed my hands under the faucet to get the soap off without fully scrubbing. *Mason.* I lunged for the paper towels and wiped down my hands.

It's him.

Not waiting for a response, I darted to the door. Mason was checking on Alvin. If Alvin had hit the flu-like-symptoms stage of hunger, I didn't know what Mason would be walking into. I pelted across the lobby, pushing past a few stragglers who were still leaving the theater. My feet pounded against the floor as I raced across the room. I flung back the curtain, revealing a winding staircase.

Mason knocked on a door just out of sight at the top of the stairs. "Alvin? Come on, man. I know you're in there. I can hear you. Are you all right?"

I scrambled up the steps. "Stop!"

"Alvin? Come on, man." A key scraped against a doorknob. "I'm coming in."

I swung around the turn in the stairs as Mason turned the key.

"Wait!" I yelled.

The door to Alvin's apartment swung inward. The room was almost pitch-black. Something growled, and a pale hand darted through the doorway, grabbed Mason by the throat, and pulled him inside.

# CHAPTER 19

I sprinted up the stairs and threw myself into the darkened room. Thick blackout curtains covered the windows. I blindly reached out, took Mason's arm, and yanked him back. As he stumbled, one of the curtains slid in his grasp, and a small beam of light fell on Alvin's face, which turned to me, eyes wide and bloodshot. There was no recognition in his gaze. His dark-brown hair stuck up in all directions as if he'd been pulling on it. His jeans were torn and his T-shirt stained with sweat. He pulled his lips back in a snarl and flung himself forward, grabbing for me.

"Stop!" I pushed magic into the word. Petals swarmed around Alvin, blanketing him in red.

Growling past the petals, he scrambled to me then seized my arms and pulled me farther into the room. I flung my other arm wide, patting the wall in search of a shelf, a movie poster—anything I could hold onto or chuck at him. My fingers slipped along the drywall as he dragged me farther into his apartment.

Mason screamed behind me, "What the heck? What's happening? What's wrong with him? Is it contagious?"

I dug my heels in and leaned back. "Run! Get out of here! Call the sheriff."

Mason careened onto the landing behind me. I lost track of him as I continued the tug-of-war over my arm with Alvin.

Verbal commands weren't working. I poured more magic into the air. "*Calm* down."

He pulled harder, wrenching me forward into his grasp. His hands clawed at me as he growled mindlessly into my face, foaming at the mouth. I pushed up on his chin to keep his snapping teeth away from me.

"Call the sheriff!" I shouted.

I couldn't hear Mason anymore. I didn't know if he'd made it to the stairs or if help was coming. The muscles in my arms screamed at me as I held him back with all my strength. I pictured Mason's face, and the face of every patron who had been loitering in the lobby, as I pushed against him.

*He can't leave this room.*

My enchantment specialization was useless against him. But my second strongest school of magic was transmutation. I shrieked, and another wave of petals left me, coating my arms and chest in red. I pictured a silverback gorilla. When I was a kid, I'd seen one toss a broken tree trunk across its enclosure at the Woodland Park Zoo. I gritted my teeth, my muscles tightening and reforming under the skin. I pushed against him, putting everything I had into the shove. He flew backward and hit the far wall.

I turned and rushed to the door as the transformation of my body melted away. I bumbled onto the landing, my limbs heavy. Mason stood there, his eyes wide and staring. I pushed him toward the stairs then spun in place to slam the door. I could hear Alvin launching himself against it on the other side. The door rattled, the wood splintering. I pushed my hands into the wood and muttered the words to a containment spell. Normally, I would use enchantment magic to make people want to stay away. But appealing to Alvin's emotions didn't seem to work. He was too far gone. The door jolted under my touch. I ignored it and continued on, muttering the words to another spell. I layered five spells on the doorway to strengthen it and to keep Alvin on the other side.

"What was that? What's wrong with him?" Mason babbled from his spot on the stairs. He had collapsed against the wall and was hugging his knees.

I crouched next to him and touched his chin then tipped his head back until he met my eyes. "It's going to be okay."

Alvin thudded against the wall again. Plaster cracked around the door. I pushed myself to my feet and put my hands on the walls. I murmured the words to a few more spells, spreading the reinforcement of the wood into the walls around it. My stomach growled as the last words left my mouth. I sagged against the wall then stumbled a few feet down the steps.

Mason peered up at me. "What's wrong with you?"

"I'm okay," I lied.

When I reached for my backpack, my hand hit empty air. I pressed my forehead against the wall. I had left it in the bathroom. I desperately needed to refuel, but the closest food was at the bottom of the stairs.

Mason stood and steadied me. "You don't look like you're feeling well. You didn't catch what he has, did you?"

I shook my head. "Low blood sugar."

He walked down the stairs as if in a daze. "I'll grab you a soda."

The door shuddered behind me as I took my first step down. I glanced behind me. The wood cracked and split. Alvin peered at me through the sliver. He snarled, foam spilling from his mouth.

"Run!" I pushed Mason ahead of me.

My limbs were uncoordinated as I tumbled after him down the steps. I was too exhausted to cast another containment spell, and my body was too confused to move correctly. I hadn't had the time or energy to properly transition my arms back, so they had returned to normal on their own, which left my nerve endings muddled. I didn't dare waste what little energy I had left on looking back or trying to fix it. We hit the lobby as the last group of moviegoers exited the auditorium into the lobby. Wood splintered overhead, and footsteps thundered down the stairs.

I wavered at the bottom of the stairs. There was no way any of them would be able to protect themselves from what was coming. I turned toward the doorway and held up my hands. Three small petals hung in the air before dissipating into nothing.

Alvin launched himself from the doorway, throwing himself at me. Victor slammed into him midair and grappled him to the floor. I stared for half a second as they wrestled with each other. Then I stumbled back and grabbed the first box of candy I could find. I ripped it open and dumped a large mouthful of Nerds into my mouth. My tongue tingled as the sour and sweet went down my throat. As I guzzled the candy, Victor and Alvin rolled together behind the counter.

"Stay back!" I motioned the group of curious moviegoers away before swallowing the last mouthful of Nerds and seizing another box. Staggering behind the counter, I shook more candy down my throat.

Victor and Alvin rolled back and forth, popcorn clinging to their clothes. My hands shook. Victor, sweat streaming off his face, had Alvin pinned, but his fingers were slipping. Alvin bit into his arm. The sugar had barely done anything to my magic reserves, but I had to do something. Anything.

I dropped down and pressed my hands against the wooden floorboards. I poured what little magic I had left in my system into the floor. The boards heaved under the two men, the wood warping and reforming into vines as it wrapped around Alvin.

I collapsed backward and stared as Victor held him in place. The wooden vines restricted Alvin's movements. He flopped around, desperately snapping his jaws.

Victor shoved him down. "We just have to hold on until help arrives."

"Help?" I asked.

Alvin bucked against him. Victor grunted, and his hands slipped. "She's on her way."

"Who?"

A beam of pure white light snaked around the counter and enveloped Alvin. I blinked. A small laugh escaped me. Miranda was here. The Warden who had made my life difficult since the day she arrived was saving me.

Alvin stilled as the white light covered him completely and Miranda stepped around the counter into view. "I'll take it from here," she said. "Alvin Stokes, you are under arrest."

I fell back against the counter. My arms felt like noodles as I raised them to a pull box of candy from the shelves behind the counter. I glanced at the box. Chocolate-covered raisins. Everything was better with chocolate.

Miranda dragged Alvin away as I ate. "Are you going to be to containing this?" She gestured to the small group of patrons huddled against the back wall.

I shrugged. "If you get them to stay for a bit. I just need to eat some more."

She nodded. "If you need help, call me. I can haul them all in to be processed elsewhere."

My stomach lurched at the idea of them sitting in holding cells. Their families would be worried. I shook my head.

Miranda shrugged. Before leaving, she sealed the doors.

Mason and the patrons pressed themselves against the wall. There were six in total. They stared as I made my way through four boxes of candy, a bucket of butter-coated popcorn, and a large Coke. With each bite and sip, my energy slowly returned.

Victor leaned against the counter, watching me. "That's an impressive appetite you've got there."

I snorted. "You have no idea how much energy magic takes. I'm going to need a full steak dinner, baked potatoes, and all the fixings after this."

"With bacon and cheese?"

I let out an exhausted chuckle. "I did say all the fixings."

Victor handed me a large pretzel. I tore it apart as I studied the other people in the room. It had taken me so long to regain my energy that they'd begun to fluctuate between fear and exhaustion.

Once my hands steadied, I straightened and walked over to the mundane humans who had witnessed the strange events. One by one, I muttered the words to the spell that would let me alter their thoughts. I made a few simple changes. Alvin had gotten into an altercation with what appeared to be someone's jealous boyfriend. The mundane humans didn't want to get involved, so they'd left. They heard Alvin was leaving town for a bit to avoid the fallout.

Mason was the last one. He shoved his hands into his pockets. "I feel like I'm about to be flashy thinged. You know —from *Men in Black*."

I smiled at him. "Sort of."

"Does it hurt?"

"No."

He sighed. "The coolest thing I've ever seen, and I'm not going to remember it. Before you do it, though, can I just tell you—thank you. It was all so crazy that I just kind of froze. I know you saved me."

My stomach clenched. Sometimes being a witch who was good at altering memories sucked. Mason was sweet. But containment was my job. I snapped my fingers in front of him, and told him the same story I'd given everyone else. His gaze was blank as he swayed in place, his new memories settling in his mind. I snapped my fingers, releasing him, and hobbled to the door.

Victor followed me out and wrapped an arm around my shoulders. Come Monday, I was going to have a lot to explain to the city council. But for the moment, I needed to eat more and then sleep.

# CHAPTER 20

Gertie shifted under me as we rode into town. My nerves over my impending report to Edgar had gotten the better of me that morning, and I couldn't bear to leave her behind. Through our familiar bond, she sent me calming emotions. She trudged to a stop outside city hall, and I stroked her neck before dismounting and sliding down to the ground.

The lobby was vacant when I walked inside. I strode down the hall to the council room, my head held high. When I entered, everyone else was already there. Seated at the long table in the back, staring at me expectantly, were the councilors. They sat in their usual positions, with Arthur on the far left followed by Helen, Steven, Edgar, Mandy, and Nicholas. On my side of the banister, seated in the pews next to each other, were Chris, Victor, and Miranda. It was a closed-door session, and my coven mates had not been invited.

My palms became sweaty as I made my way to the banister and the small podium where constituents were allowed to stand and offer their opinions. The room was silent.

"So nice of you to finally join us," Edgar said.

My gaze flicked to the clock on the back wall. I was a minute early. I forced a professional smile onto my face and gripped the podium.

"We've heard some curious things over the weekend." Edgar pulled a sheaf of paper from a file in front of him. "Miranda submitted an incident report. I don't see one from you."

I cleared my throat. "I thought it best to present my findings in person."

"You mean your justifications." Edgar slammed the paper down.

Nicholas leaned forward, reaching across Mandy to push Edgar back into his seat. "I read the incident report too. You're overreacting."

Edgar's eye twitched. "She continued investigating when—"

"When we made the wrong decision." Nicholas smirked. "Obviously."

"That doesn't give her the right—" Edgar spluttered.

"Let the girl speak." Arthur cleaned his glasses with the cloth. "I, for one, found the incident report lacking."

I glanced behind me. Miranda didn't turn her head. She continued to stare straight ahead, not meeting my eye. *What did she write in there?*

I turned back to the city council. "When I was here last, I didn't get a chance to finish my case update before it was taken away from me."

Steven raised his eyebrow.

Nicholas's smile widened. "Told you."

"My interview with Ethan revealed that he is some sort of memory sponge psychic. He soaked up the memories of the attacker. I used magic to access his memories. And with his memories—where I could *clearly* see the hands that assaulted Mr. Perez were not Ethan's—combined with the statement from the ghost, I was able to determine that the attacker was a vampire."

Helen and Arthur nodded along.

"Knowing that Ethan was going to be arraigned on Monday and that it was not a slam dunk case, as he was retracting his statement, I opted to continue with my job. I interviewed Manual's child, which led me back to Mr. Stokes. It became clear soon after I arrived at the movie theater that Mr. Stokes was the responsible party. And with the help of Miranda, he was detained."

"He has been transferred to the Wardens' facility in Wyoming," Miranda said.

"Why did he do it?" Mandy asked.

I tried to keep my expression as blank as possible. "He seems to have been cut off from his food source and was hungry."

"Food source? Is this a safety concern?" Helen asked.

"I... I don't think so. Vampires aren't typically violent." My hands clenched, my fingernails digging into the wood. "I suspect this is an isolated incident."

"And if you hadn't been there to question Alvin, what would have happened?" Nicholas asked.

"I suspect he would have attacked others," I said.

Chris spoke up behind me. "The theater is close to the bookstore. He most likely wandered there in search of food. We may have been looking at a repeat incident. And given the time of day, it would have been ten times worse."

Nicholas tipped back in his seat. "Told you guys we should have let her finish her investigation. I think she should be commended for thinking ahead."

Edgar scoffed. "I think she should be fired for failing to follow directions."

Steven sighed. "Are either of those formal motions?"

"Yes," both men said at the same time.

A stone settled in my stomach, my vision narrowing to

their faces. When I first got the position of liaison, I hadn't wanted it. But this was the second time an innocent person would have been blamed if I hadn't been involved.

"All right. Does anyone second the motion to commend her?"

No one spoke.

I bit down on the inside of my cheek to keep the panic from showing on my face.

"Does anyone second the motion to fire her?" Steven looked left and right.

Again, no one spoke.

"It looks like neither motion has sufficient backing to make it to the floor." Steven nodded. "All right. Unless there were any further questions, I think this concludes our meeting."

Helen stood and gathered up her knitting from the floor. "Good. I need to go pick my grandbabies up. I get to babysit tonight."

I sank onto the pew behind me as everyone filtered out of the room, chatting with each other. Chris patted my shoulder on his way out. Before too long, I was left with Victor. He stood back, waiting for me to collect my thoughts.

My coven was meeting me at the Slice of Life diner for an update. The last time I'd spoken with them, I had been a few pointed questions away from losing my job. Fortunately, Chris had spoken up for me, and I appeared to have an ally in Nicholas.

I stood and trudged out of the meeting room, with Victor in tow.

He smiled at the sight of Gertie. "I should have guessed you would have your best friend with you today."

I patted her shoulder and took her reins. "Yeah. She's my rock."

"Where are you off to next?"

"Lunch with my coven."

He nodded and took a step back.

"Did you want to join us?" The question came out before I had a chance to fully think it over.

He smiled. "I would love to. Did you want to walk? It's a beautiful day."

I agreed, and we turned together. The Slice of Life diner was only a few minutes away on foot. We meandered down the street side-by-side, with Gertie trailing a few feet behind us. Her hooves clopped against the sidewalk, and she paused every few feet to sniff at different things.

"Thank you," Victor said.

I glanced at him. "I was just doing my job."

"You did more than that."

My palms became sweaty. I patted Gertie's shoulder to give me something to do with my hands. "Oh?"

"You kept my secret."

"I..." My mind went blank. The only thought left in my head was that I'd given him my word. "We pinky promised."

"They really are binding with you, aren't they?"

I nodded.

He stopped in the middle of the sidewalk and turned to me. Gertie and I followed suit. I tilted my chin back as he captured my gaze with his. He held his hand up, his pinky sticking out.

"What's this?" I asked.

"Another pinky promise."

I giggled and linked my pinky with his. "What are we promising?"

"*I'm* promising to never doubt you again."

I blinked.

He squeezed my pinky with his. "It's hard, you know? For over a hundred years, I've been trained to always look for the ulterior motive. To expect the worst. I promise not to do that with you."

"Oh." I didn't know what to say. "Thank you?"

Victor chuckled and pulled me into a one-armed hug. I hugged him back. We pulled apart and continued our slow progression to the diner. Gertie's plodding pace turned the three-minute walk into a ten-minute one. By the time we reached the diner, I had a smile on my face from my conversation with Victor, and the tension from the grilling Edgar had put me through had lifted.

We stopped so I could position Gertie in a parking spot. I put down my usual yellow cones to warn people that she was there on purpose and turned to go inside. Victor ground to a halt next to me, and dropped to his knee in a low bow. I almost stumbled over him.

I lunged to the side at the last second. "Victor?"

He kept his head bowed. I looked around. It was past the usual lunch rush, and there was hardly anyone on the street. The only person even close by was a teenage boy wearing surfer pants and a loose white T-shirt. His dark hair was pulled into a messy bun on the top of his head.

"What are you doing?" I whispered.

"You may stand." The boy glided forward.

Victor rose but kept his gaze lowered.

"You may go ahead inside. I just wanted a word with your friend first." The boy's voice was even, but the way the words were pronounced was odd. I couldn't place the accent. It was like all his vowels were distinct.

"Of course, My King." Victor glanced my way, an apology in his eyes, before he turned and disappeared inside.

*My King?* I instinctively pulled myself straighter. My expression became blank. Every single lesson my mother had ever taught me about looking confident and not turning myself into a target ran through my mind.

The boy stepped closer. He met my gaze. There was something ancient in his eyes. "For the purposes of this conversation, you may call me Kai."

"Kai?"

He nodded.

"But first, before we begin our conversation in earnest, you must introduce me to your familiar. It has been a long time since I've seen something as unusual as a cow being chosen."

I ground my teeth and stepped toward my familiar. I put a protective hand over her shoulder. "Her name's Gertie."

He stepped close and held out his hand so she could sniff his fingers. "She has a curious soul. I can feel it. Does she enjoy adventures?"

My hand relaxed on her shoulder. "She does."

"I always enjoy the more interesting choices." He stroked the side of her face. "I suspect we will get along well."

"What did you want to speak with me about?"

"It is a private matter. I expect I can trust your discretion."

My mouth felt dry. Another promise. Another private matter. I nodded, words failing me.

"Alvin was my youngest. He fed on fear." Kai leveled his gaze on me. "He operated a movie theater that played horror films daily. It should not have been possible for him to starve."

"Okay..."

Kai stepped closer to me. With him only a foot away, I could see black tattoos poking out from the neck of his shirt. The design appeared geometric. "I have not seen anything new in a long time. I have not been surprised by anything in centuries. Normally, I would be overjoyed at encountering something new and unexplained. This does not bring me joy."

"All right... why are you telling me this?"

He inched forward. My vision filled with his dark-brown eyes. I couldn't look away.

"You're an investigator, are you not?" His voice lulled me forward.

I leaned toward him, nodding.

"And I am a man in need of answers. Will you find them for me?"

"Yes." It was like the promise had been pulled from my chest. I couldn't fight the answer. It slipped out unbidden.

"Excellent, Megan. I can call you Megan, correct?"

I nodded.

"Wonderful. Find me my answers, Megan, and I will overlook my son being harmed by you."

My whole body shook, but I couldn't look away. His dark-brown eyes burrowed into my mind.

"Are we agreed, Megan? Answers for forgiveness?"

I nodded.

He stepped back, and I sagged against Gertie's side.

"Excellent." He turned on his heel. "Enjoy your lunch, Megan."

The king walked away, his stride languid. I stared at his back until he turned and disappeared around the corner. I shuddered and stroked Gertie's side for comfort. Then I wiped my sweaty palms against my jeans and made my way inside, where my friends were waiting. I had made a lot of promises over the last week, but I had a feeling the one to the king would be the hardest to keep.

---

Ready for the next enchanting adventure? You can pre-order Book 3, 'Murder Under the Moon,' here.

In book 3, Megan Miller is beginning to understand that life as Point Pleasant's supernatural liaison is anything but predictable. When Travis Burrow, leader of the local werewolf pack, comes to her for help, Megan knows this isn't just another case. A member of his pack has been accused of murder, and the Wardens of the West aren't taking chances. They've started rounding up every werewolf in town.

With their freedom on the line, Megan doesn't have the luxury of easing into the investigation.

The victim was newly married into the pack—and recently hired to design a controversial housing development already dividing the community. As Megan digs deeper, she finds herself caught between small-town politics and shifter traditions that don't welcome outside interference. Everyone has something to protect. Everyone has a reason to lie.

With tensions rising and the clock ticking, Megan must uncover the truth before suspicion turns into something far more permanent. Justice in Point Pleasant isn't always simple… and sometimes getting it wrong costs more than one life.

Perfect for fans of witchy small towns, found family, and cozy mysteries with a magical twist, this paranormal cozy will keep you guessing until the very end.

## ALSO BY ELOISE EVERHART

### A Williams Witch Mystery

Potions and the Pleasantly Poisoned

Tomes and the Tangled Trail

Divinations and the Disappearing Dead

Hexes and the Haunted House

Spells and the Suspiciously Silent

Grimoires and the Ghostly Guest

Enchantments and the Eerily Ensnared

Rituals and the Restless Remains

Charms and the Cursed Coven

### A Miller's Magical Mystery

Murder Among the Hives

Murder Between the Stacks

Murder Under the Moon

# JOIN MY NEWSLETTER

Curious to see how what Harriet Spellman's Field Guide looks like? Join our mailing list for exclusive updates and receive access to the completed field guide entries.

# ABOUT THE AUTHOR

Eloise Everhart lives in the Pacific Northwest. Her childhood was marked by voracious reading and tabletop roleplaying games, fueling her lifelong passion for storytelling.

By day, she's a dedicated insurance adjuster. It's a career that has honed her sharp eye for detail and developed her inquisitive mind—a skillset she now seamlessly integrates into her cozy mystery writing.

Beyond her storytelling ardor, Eloise is a devoted wife, sharing her home with a menagerie of rescued cats and dogs who have found their furever home in the Everhart household.

# ACKNOWLEDGMENTS

I can't believe I'm done with the second book in this series already. There's something both comforting and challenging about returning to a world and characters I love, and once again, this book would not be what it is without the support of the people around me.

To my editors, Rashida Breen and Sarah Carleton, thank you for helping me shape this story into what it needed to be. You always know when to encourage me to slow down and let the quieter moments breathe, and your insight adds so much depth and heart to every book.

To my beloved husband, Nate, I don't think I could have made it through this past year without you. You are my rock in every sense of the word. Your constant support, patience, and belief in me keep me moving forward, even on the days when the words feel hard to find. I am so incredibly lucky to have you.

To my sister, Andrea, thank you for always being in my corner. Your support never wavers, and it means more than I can say. To my father, Chas, and my mother, Tammy, your encouragement continues to give me strength. I am so grateful for your love and support.

And as always, I would like to give a special thanks to someone who is no longer with us, Andrew Henderson. For years you were my writing partner, my confidant, and my greatest friend. I will forever be grateful that you made me start writing again. I carry your memory with me always.

"Come on a journey with me."

www.ingramcontent.com/pod-product-compliance
Lightning Source LLC
LaVergne TN
LVHW051002080826
845145LV00009B/2417

* 9 7 8 1 9 6 2 7 5 9 1 0 6 *